5015 9036

# THE
# STONE
# GIRL

# THE
# STONE
# GIRL

ALYSSA B. SHEINMEL

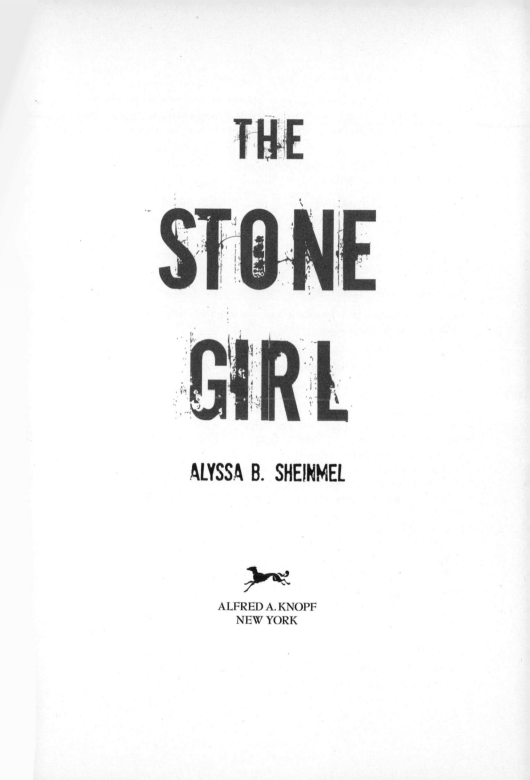

ALFRED A. KNOPF
NEW YORK

Text copyright © 2012 by Alyssa B. Sheinmel
Jacket art copyright © 2012 by Zhang Jingna

All rights reserved. Published in the United States by Alfred A. Knopf, an imprint of Random House Children's Books, a division of Random House, Inc., New York.

Knopf, Borzoi Books, and the colophon are registered trademarks of Random House, Inc.

Visit us on the Web! randomhouse.com/teens

Educators and librarians, for a variety of teaching tools, visit us at RHTeachersLibrarians.com

*Library of Congress Cataloging-in-Publication Data*
The stone girl / Alyssa B. Sheinmel. — 1st ed.
p.   cm.
Summary: Seventeen-year-old Sethie, a senior at New York City's Franklin White girl's school, has outstanding grades, a boyfriend, and a new best friend but constantly struggles to lose weight.
ISBN 978-0-375-87080-4 (trade) — ISBN 978-0-375-97080-1 (lib. bdg.) — ISBN 978-0-307-97462-4 (ebook)
[1. Anorexia nervosa—Fiction. 2. Eating disorders—Fiction. 3. Dating (Social customs)—Fiction. 4. Friendship—Fiction. 5. Schools—Fiction. 6. Mothers and daughters—Fiction. 7. New York (N.Y.)—Fiction.] I. Title.
PZ7.S54123Sto 2012
[Fic]—dc23
2011037768

The text of this book is set in 12-point Dutch 766.

Printed in the United States of America
August 2012
10 9 8 7 6 5 4 3 2 1

First Edition

THIS BOOK IS FOR
ELAINE S. B. SHEINMEL.

**IT IS SEPTEMBER** in New York City and Sarah Beth Weiss has just turned seventeen. For as long as she can remember, she has been called Sethie; her parents, her grandparents, even cousins and uncles who barely know her name at all, know that she is called Sethie. Only new teachers get it wrong. At school, when they go through roll call, Sethie has always had to interrupt to explain. It happened just today, the first day of her senior year. She thought all the teachers at her small school would know her real name by now. But there was a new math teacher today. It wasn't his fault, and Sethie knows it, but she was angry at him. She was frustrated that he made her explain about her name. She felt bad, later, for having been angry.

Sethie is rushing. She goes to an all-girls school, the Franklin White School, or the White School, or White for short, a name whose irony—or complete lack thereof—is lost on none of the homogenous student body. School has ended for the day, and all Sethie can think about is the boy, the boy, the boy. All summer long, she didn't have to wait until three-fifteen to see him, and now she can't remember how she managed before. And she remembers waiting even longer, last year, when she had yearbook editorial meetings that lasted past five, or appointments with her SAT tutor at the coffee shop after school.

Shaw, Shaw, Shaw. She sings it to herself, rushing, like a horse being taunted with a carrot on a stick—must get that carrot, must go faster, must get to Shaw.

There are two things that are true about Sethie: one is that she is always hungry, a mean, angry kind of hunger that feels like a piece of glass in her belly; the other is that she is always missing Shaw.

When Shaw says her name, Sethie feels it on her skin. Her name sounds serious coming out of his mouth, in his deep voice, a voice that belongs somewhere else—in an opera house, on a film screen, coming out of the radio. A voice that deserves to be anywhere but on her bedroom floor, actually speaking to her, paying attention to her, saying her name. Giving her name heft it never had before.

Shaw, Shaw, Shaw. The name that feels like it never finishes, like it's missing a letter at the end. She knows that he can't have missed her all day, not the way she has missed him. Shaw would never be bothered with missing anyone. Shaw doesn't believe in relying on someone else for his own happiness. Shaw's friends were mostly away all summer; he probably actually enjoyed his first day back at school, probably enjoyed seeing all of those other people, getting new books, pressing freshly sharpened pencils into loose-leaf paper.

Sethie knows Shaw's pencils are freshly sharpened, because last night she cleaned out his school bag. Shaw was in the shower, and she threw away all his chewed-up and worn-down pencils and replaced them with fresh ones of her own. A surprise for his first day back.

Sethie has approached this whole day with speed, rushing from class to class, running up and down the stairs, watching the clock, willing it to be eighth period. The other girls walked slowly between classes, catching up, complaining about this or that teacher, agonizing over college applications. Sethie arrived to each class early, turned to the first page of her notebook, and pressed her pen to the top of the page, ready to get on with things. Her classmates sat in the senior lounge; they'd waited years for that lounge, long and skinny, with doors to close the teachers out. It's very small; Sethie thinks that at another school, it might be too small to fit the entire senior class inside it. But all the girls at Sethie's school are skinny. Since most of the girls have been there since kindergarten, Sethie imagines the application process. No overly-sturdy-looking four-year-olds would have been considered.

The most exciting thing about the senior lounge is that it has a pay phone in it. All the girls have been waiting for it since they began attending White and were faced with the faculty's rigid no-cell-phone policy. Sethie remembers what a big deal it was when she was ten years old and her mother finally let her have a cell phone; having the pay phone in the senior lounge seems just as exciting. Sethie still has that same cell phone, in a box under her bed. Sometimes she recharges it and looks at the old text messages she and her friends sent each other in fifth grade. Today, Sethie's classmates all called the boys they like at other schools to give them the number to the senior lounge. The phone rang all day. Sethie has decided she won't give Shaw the number. That way it won't bother her when he doesn't call.

Sethie knows that for all of her rushing today, all of her running from class to class, Shaw has been strolling. Shaw takes his time. Shaw does not rush.

It's one of the things Sethie likes about him. He never worries about being late; he gets to the places he's going when he's ready to be there, and so it's always the right time. She would love to feel that kind of calm, would love to crawl up inside him for a day and feel what it's like to be inside that body: so assured, so smooth, so taut, so lean, and so slow. Shaw doesn't have to rush for her, after all—she does enough rushing for the both of them.

When Sethie finally sees him, Shaw isn't waiting for her. He's on the corner with his friends, but he's not waiting. Had they discussed that she would meet him after school? She thought they had, but now he looks so surprised to see her that she thinks maybe not; maybe she just decided she would come here, and now she's just lucky that Shaw is here.

"Hey, kiddo," he says, and she stands next to him. He does not kiss her hello. He does not put an arm around her.

4

To show she is his, she takes his cigarette from him, and takes a long drag from it.

Shaw's school, Houseman Prep, is coed, so the circle on the corner of the block in which Sethie stands with Shaw includes girls and boys, not just girls, like the corners outside Sethie's school. All the different schools uptown are really just like one big school laid out on an enormous campus. It wouldn't even qualify as an enormous campus. Sethie bets there are some real campuses that are even bigger. In California, maybe, or in Europe.

Everyone begins walking. Sethie isn't quite sure, but she thinks they're going to her building. Sethie lives with her mother a few blocks away, and there is a vacant apartment next to theirs, one that has yet to be rented. No one locks it—the building people leave it open so the Realtors can go in and out with prospective tenants. But all summer long, it's where Sethie and Shaw went to smoke. Sethie knew, of course, that it was risky, but where else could they go? Sethie's mother works odd hours, constantly breezing into and out of the apartment, and Shaw's mother doesn't work at all, and is always home. So they went next door.

But Sethie is fairly certain she didn't invite all these people back to the vacant apartment. She only intended for the two of them to go there. She doesn't want them all back there. She only wants Shaw to come. If all of these people come, when will she and Shaw have a chance to be alone together? And will these people know they have to be quiet? Will they bring other people back again, some later time? Will they be done when she's ready to go home, or will she have to wait for them, wanting to go home, when her apartment is right next door? But she won't be able to leave, because she'll be responsible. She'll be the host. She wishes she were Shaw. Responsibility rolls down his back like water in the shower. She wishes she didn't care what anyone thought. But she knows too well that the landlord hates her mother, who is occasionally late with the rent. Sometimes he calls Sethie's father, who lives in California, for the money, as though it's the absence of a man that's making Rebecca late. But Sethie knows that like Shaw, Rebecca can't always be hampered by dates and times. Though her lateness isn't smooth the way Shaw's is. Rebecca's lateness is always messy, choppy, harried.

Sethie knows the landlord would love an excuse to evict the tenants of 12A, Rebecca and her daughter, Sethie, the quiet girl who no one would have guessed might be a troublemaker.

"Shaw?" Sethie asks, quiet, scared.

"Yeah, kiddo?"

Sethie loves when he calls her kiddo. Even though she's actually a month older than he is, he seems ages wiser.

"Where are we all going?"

"To the vacant apartment."

The vacant apartment. Not theirs. Not even hers.

"All of us?"

"Why not?" He shrugs like it's no big deal, and Sethie nods. If Shaw says it's okay, says it's safe, then it must be.

Sethie wants, more than anything, more than kisses, more than sex, more than drugs, to take Shaw's hand just then. Actually, she would prefer Shaw take hers, but she'd settle for taking his. But he's never, not once, held her hand. Not even while they were messing around. So she cannot take his. He's never done anything to let her know that holding hands is okay. She imagines what it would be like if Shaw took her hand. He would do it so casually, so weightlessly, the way he did everything else. He would hold her hand like it was nothing: light as air, fluid as water. She would feel his skin against hers intensely, want to hold tighter, dig her nails in, press her fingertips against the bones on the back of his hand. But he would hold her hand loosely. He would drop her hand if she squeezed too tight. If she hurt him.

Someday he'll take her hand. Sethie can wait. When your boyfriend is someone who's always late and you're someone who's always early, you become good at waiting. *Boyfriend.* Sethie rolls the word around inside her mouth. She can't say it out loud. Instead she enjoys the feel of it on her tongue, between her teeth, filling up her mouth until she has to swallow it whole to keep it from escaping.

They haven't stopped walking, and soon they are in Sethie's lobby. How many people are here? Sethie looks around. Four people, plus her and Shaw. Four isn't so bad, she reasons. Four people won't get her in too much trouble. She only knows two of the others. Three boys and one girl. Sethie likes it that this feels like a boys' thing to do— sneak into an apartment, smoke pot, evade adult capture. In the elevator, Sethie holds her wrist. When she is nervous, Sethie wraps the fingers of one hand around the opposite wrist. She finds her wrists reassuring: this is how thin she could be, if she only just really applied herself.

It's hot inside the apartment. No air-conditioning, windows closed. It's the first week of September, but August hasn't given up yet. Sethie thinks that August is like summer's bitter older sister—everyone looks forward to June and July, but by August, they want summer's refreshing half brother, September. No one longs for August by the time it rolls around. And then August doesn't even have the good manners to leave on time.

Bitch, Sethie thinks with satisfaction.

The heat doesn't bother her, since she knows it won't last long. Smoking pot always makes Sethie cold, and today is no exception. After the pipe has been passed around, the effect Sethie feels most acutely is the air upon her skin, making the hairs on her arms lift, making her shiver. She wants to get closer to Shaw, curl up beside him, but Shaw's skin is always cool to the touch, so it wouldn't make her warmer. Sethie sits on the floor. She refuses the pipe when it is passed to her a third time. The floor is hard underneath her, but Sethie likes that, since it means she's skinny today. It means the fat on her ass isn't thick enough to protect her from the wooden floor. In a while, she rolls over so that she is lying on her stomach, propped up on her elbows. She lies like this mostly so that she can feel her hip bones against the floor, hard like rocks, leaving bruises.

They aren't being quiet. Sethie looks to Shaw for help. Surely Shaw knows they're being too loud, right? But Shaw is laughing along with them. Maybe they're not too loud.

Maybe it's the pot, making her hearing sensitive, just like it does her skin.

She presses her hands against the floor and stands up. Leans against the wall that separates her apartment from this one. Her bedroom is right on the other side. She puts her ear to the wall, as if somehow that will tell her whether the noises they are all making are detectable from her own apartment on the other side.

"What are you doing, Sethie?" the other girl asks from the floor, watching.

Sethie flushes, embarrassed. She doesn't know this girl's name.

"Just listening. That's my bedroom, on the other side."

"But why would there be sounds coming from your bedroom when you're here with us?"

Sethie shrugs. "I don't know. I was just trying to figure out how loud we were being."

The girl stands up, comes over, and leans her ear against the wall. Sethie wishes she knew her name.

"Are you worried we're being too loud?"

Sethie isn't scared to tell her the truth. "Yes. I don't want my mom to get in trouble." Sethie wonders whether this sentence sounds strange: she knows it should be the other way around.

The girl laughs, but quietly. Then she turns to the four boys on the floor, even to Shaw.

"Hey, guys." They all look up at her. Sethie is impressed by the way she commands the room, this girl without a name. She's wearing jeans and a tank top, and her skin is covered in a slick of sweat, but her clothes don't stick to her skin; she's so skinny that the tank top hangs off of her shoulders, like her bones are merely hooks for the straps. Sethie is deeply aware of the ill-fitting kilt pressing against her waist—her school uniform, fitted to her in the ninth grade, a constant reminder that her body has gotten bigger since she was a freshman. It was too small even when she bought it; she'd wanted it short and hadn't quite realized that a smaller size meant tighter, not shorter. Every day when she gets dressed, she wishes she'd bought a bigger size and just rolled it, the way all the other girls in her class seemed to know how to do. She's jealous that Shaw's school doesn't require uniforms and this nameless girl gets to wear new clothes that fit her seventeen-year-old body. Not that it looks like this girl's body has changed since ninth grade like Sethie's has: there is no new roundness in her hips or her breasts, those soft spots that seemed to develop on girls like Sethie somewhere between freshman and senior year.

"We should bolt," the girl says. "It's not fair to Sethie to stay here too long."

Sethie looks at her, impressed. Then at Shaw, to see his reaction.

"All right, chickadees," Shaw says, getting up, wiping nonexistent dust from his pants. "Let's get going. Don't want to get Sethie in trouble."

For just a second, Sethie is angry. Or maybe embarrassed. Shaw has blamed her for ruining the fun. Sethie should never have said anything to the girl who sweats but doesn't get sticky. But Sethie's anxiety doesn't last long, because she realizes that if everyone leaves, Shaw might stay, come with her next door, into her own apartment. They might be alone together.

But he doesn't stay. Each of the five others kisses her on the cheek good-bye as they wait for the elevator; Shaw's kiss is last, and he lingers so she can feel his breath on her, a burst of air she feels not only on her face but all the way down to her feet. It even makes her ankles tingle. Then he leaves with the others, into the hallway, down the elevator, through the lobby, out the door. Sethie doesn't like being stoned alone. She goes to her room and curls under her covers and tries to get warm. Her teeth chatter.

She forces herself out of bed and into the kitchen. It is time for her to chug her water. Every night, Sethie must drink one liter of cold water in under twenty minutes, and she is not allowed to pee until she's finished the bottle. The water brings the coldness under her skin into her belly. She stays under the covers. She waits to use the bathroom. She steadies the chatter of her teeth. Soon, she'll be sober, and the air will feel warm again.

**SETHIE COULDN'T TELL** you when she began drinking her water every night. She doesn't remember why she's not allowed to use the bathroom until the bottle is empty. She knows the water has to be cold, because cold water is supposed to burn calories; your body uses energy to keep you warm. She read that on a Web site called anorexicnation.com, before it was blocked, or taken down, or whatever they do to Web sites like that.

Inside her room, Sethie picks up the notebook next to her bed. She calls it her journal, but it's really a list of what she eats every day. She began keeping the notebook six months ago. She writes everything down; even pieces of gum (five calories) and sips of coffee. She considers writing that Shaw didn't kiss her today, not once, not really, but she's too embarrassed.

She hears the locks in the front door turning; her mother is home.

"Hi, honey!" Rebecca calls out.

"Studying!" Sethie replies; Rebecca won't interrupt her if she thinks Sethie's working. Rebecca is very proud to have a daughter, Sethie thinks, with such good grades.

"Okay, honey," Rebecca says, and Sethie can hear her walking through the apartment; she can hear the buttons of Rebecca's jacket tapping against a dining room chair when Rebecca folds it over the back, can hear Rebecca's shoes hitting the floor when she takes them off in the living room. Sethie likes communicating with her mother with the bedroom door closed between them.

"There are leftovers in the fridge," Rebecca calls. She doesn't cook, but a few times a week she has dinners with the lawyers at the firm where she works. They usually go to steak houses, and Rebecca always orders the filet, and she always brings half of it home for Sethie. Sethie never eats it; her mother orders her meat rare. At restaurants, she tells waiters "mooing," which both embarrasses and disgusts Sethie. By the time Rebecca brings the meat home, it's cold, and looks raw. When Sethie used to try to eat it, she could barely swallow it. Rebecca doesn't seem to notice that after a couple of days, the meat disappears from the fridge because Sethie has thrown it away, not eaten it. Rebecca doesn't seem to notice that at restaurants Sethie orders meat well-done.

Sethie is still slightly stoned when she begins her homework. Last year, before she began seeing Shaw, Sethie always began her homework earlier; she never waited until just before bed, and she was certainly never stoned while she did it. Tonight, she's surprised how easy it is to read a history textbook stoned, sitting up in bed, balancing her water bottle between her knees.

There are rules for Sethie's water, other than that it must be cold. Sethie must finish the entire bottle in fewer than twenty minutes. She may not pee until she has drunk the entire bottle, no matter how much her body wants to. She must always drink her water before eight-thirty; if she finishes later than eight-thirty, she'll still have to pee later, when it's time to go to bed. Still, every morning, she wakes up and can barely make it to the bathroom. It's usually the urge to urinate that wakes her, in fact. She doesn't even need an alarm clock, though she always sets one.

Before Sethie falls asleep, she imagines what she will eat the next day. Every new day, Sethie thinks, is an opportunity to be good. Lying in bed, Sethie imagines the clean slate of a day spread out for tomorrow; when she closes her eyes, she sees an enormous empty plate. She plans exactly what she will eat. Sethie doesn't mind going to bed hungry; planning for the next day is more exciting that way. She imagines how satisfied her belly will be when she fills it with exactly the right amounts of only the things she should be eating. Tomorrow, perhaps she will wake up the kind of girl who doesn't get hungry for a snack after school, who simply forgets to eat lunch because she's so busy. Tomorrow she might wake up thinner than she woke up today.

Sethie has never been much of a breakfast eater. When she was younger, she skipped it because her mother skipped it, and it made her feel grown-up. Today, the second day of school, she allows herself a coffee from the cafeteria; the students aren't supposed to eat the food that's laid out at breakfast time—it's meant only for the teachers—but some girls always sneak it. Today, Sethie is pouring sugar (sugar is allowed; no fat and an extra bonus burst of energy) into her coffee when she overhears two juniors debating about sneaking some food.

"I think I want a corn muffin."

"So get one."

"What if I get caught?"

"Then you'll put it back."

"Anyway, I'd rather do what's healthier."

"It's healthier to take the corn muffin. Breakfast is the most important meal of the day."

The other girl rolls her eyes. "No, I mean healthier like better for my diet."

"Oh."

Sethie thinks that the teachers are hypocrites: they're always warning the girls about the dangers of dieting, but then they restrict the students' access to breakfast. Sethie remembers the taste of the corn muffins here; she stole them herself from time to time, when she was in ninth grade, maybe even in tenth. She remembers how scared she was of being caught; she was the kind of student for whom stealing muffins might be considered acting out. She remembers that they were always warm, and the way that they crumbled when she bit into them.

At lunchtime, Sethie spreads peanut butter over a bagel in the cafeteria. She is standing by the pastry table, where there are all kinds of breads so that the students can make their own sandwiches. At Sethie's school, you're not allowed to bring your own lunch. The cost of the school lunch is included in the tuition. Sethie added it up one day, and it came to something like eight dollars a meal. Not for me, Sethie thinks, balancing the bagel on a textbook; Sethie is on full scholarship. She wants to spread the peanut butter on thick, lick the leftovers from the knife. Behave, she says, almost out loud. Be good. *Half* a bagel. *Thin* layer of peanut butter. Coffee with sugar and skim milk. She must be good at lunch because there's no telling what she might have for dinner tonight. On the phone last night, Shaw said that they're going to Jane's house tonight. When he told her that, Sethie realized that Jane is the name of the girl from yesterday, the one who listened to the other side of the wall with her.

The editor of the yearbook, Dana, stands next to her at the bagel table.

"Hey," she says to Sethie. Dana reaches over Sethie for a cinnamon raisin bagel.

"Hey," Sethie says, thinking, Calories, Calories.

"You're not coming to the meeting today?"

"Can't," Sethie says. Sethie has dropped yearbook this year. Since she did it all last year, she's still going to be listed as managing editor on the masthead, and she can still put it on her college applications, so she simply doesn't see a need to keep it up anymore.

"Oh," Dana says.

Sethie shrugs and folds her bagel up inside a napkin, to take to the library. Dana, Sethie thinks, couldn't possibly understand. Dana is tall and thin. Dana can eat a whole cinnamon raisin bagel with hot, melting butter, and not gain a pound. And Dana can have two yearbook meetings a week for eight weeks straight, meetings that begin right after school, when everyone is starving and begs to order in pizza and Chinese food. Meetings that end so that you get home just in time for dinner, which you eat anyway, because the pizza or the Chinese food at the meeting was only an after-school snack. Sethie's school is filled with Danas, girls who are genetically predisposed to thinness, girls who can't possibly understand that Sethie has to work at it, that Sethie simply cannot go to yearbook meetings this semester.

**3.**

J ANE LIVES ON 72nd and Park Avenue, in one of those apartments the elevator opens right into. The floors in the foyer are marble. Her kitchen is behind a swinging door, and Jane leads the way straight there. Sethie thinks she could have found the kitchen without having been led, the smell of food in the apartment is so strong.

No one else is home. Jane is an only child, and her parents travel a lot. The housekeeper has already left for the day. The kitchen counters gleam. The air-conditioning is set so cool that it makes the room seem cleaner. The housekeeper has made sure there is enough food for everyone for dinner. Jane must have told her she was having friends over. Sethie, Jane, and Shaw gather around the island in the center of the kitchen. Sethie eyes a bowl of nuts in the middle of the island. She is waiting until someone else—Jane or Shaw, she doesn't care who—begins to eat them so that she can eat them too. If she doesn't wait for them to eat first, she will be like a pig who only came here tonight for the food.

Jane, Sethie thinks wryly, is anything but plain. She has thin blond hair to her shoulders and wears big hoop earrings, short shorts out of which pop skinny legs. Her eyes are dark with kohl, her lips bright with Vaseline. She looks, still, like she just got out of bed—but in a sexy way, as if only to remind you that her bed is close by.

"You guys woke me up," Jane says, reaching, Sethie notices gratefully, for a handful of nuts.

"We did?" Shaw asks.

"Yeah. Fell asleep watching *Taxi* reruns."

Sethie's head snaps away from the nuts to look at Jane. "I love that show," she says seriously.

Jane grins. "Me too! My dad recorded every episode back when it ran. I used to watch it sitting on his lap."

Sethie smiles back. "My dad, too. Even now, whenever I hear that music from the opening credits, I think of him."

"Me too," Jane says, and smiles, so that Sethie knows that Jane's father isn't around much, either, though perhaps for reasons more interesting than divorce. Jane hums the *Taxi* theme song, and Sethie joins in. Shaw looks at them like they're both crazy, so Sethie stops, and then Jane does, too, but she's laughing.

Sethie and Shaw went to Shaw's apartment before coming here. Shaw wanted to show her his new bong. Sethie had never smoked from a bong, and Shaw had to teach her.

"Put your hand there. Okay, now I'm going to hold the

lighter, and you inhale. Got it? Then you take the bowl out and breathe it up, just like that, good girl." Shaw was very tender. He rubbed her upper arm; he was sweet when it took several tries. And then, something caught, something worked correctly, and the smoke filled Sethie's mouth and throat. She wasn't sure whether the calm that came over her was from the pot or from having used the bong correctly.

Then Shaw took a hit. Sethie admired his expertise. He leaned in, after, and Sethie went to kiss him, thinking that it had been two whole days since they kissed and longing for his kisses, for what always came after. But she did something wrong. Shaw pulled away, his eyes red.

"You have to inhale, Sethie," he said, coughing, but not angry. He had been blowing smoke into her mouth. He hadn't been kissing her. Sethie wished she'd done it correctly. Maybe now he won't do it again. She wanted a second chance.

Shaw put the bong down, lay on his back. Sethie hesitated, then lay down next to him, but not quite touching. She always waits until he touches her first. She thought it was strange that he hadn't kissed her for two days. Maybe she could remind him, somehow, of how it's supposed to be. She felt distinctly the space between them. She waited for Shaw to reach for her, waited for him to tell her it was okay.

And then his hand went to her face, and then down, over her arms, lower, pulling her close, rubbing her back, pulling her leg over his.

It's not real unless he kisses me, Sethie thought. It doesn't count unless he kisses me.

She grabbed at him, feeling clumsy, turned her face up at him. Please kiss me, please. His hands, always cold, on her upper thighs, under her school uniform, reaching for the curve of her ass. His face, buried in the pillow, looking away. Was he teasing her? Did he know it didn't count until he kissed her?

And then, he turned, fast, and kissed her. Sethie felt relief, everywhere. She sank into the bed, curled underneath him. His mouth was always cold, his tongue always slipped between her lips like ice water. She wondered, briefly, whether it was really pot that made her cold or the fact that she only ever smoked with Shaw, the boy whose caresses would never make you warm, against whom it was pointless to lean for heat. The boy who kissed ice cubes into her mouth until she swallowed, so that the cold filled her belly. She didn't care if she was ever warm again. Sethie knows people don't end up with their high school sweethearts, not anymore, not in New York, but she also couldn't imagine ever being there with anyone but Shaw. Would anyone else ever know her body like this, know to put his thigh between her legs and rub her scalp with one hand, while grabbing her bottom with the other? She didn't even know she wanted to be touched in those places all at once until Shaw did it. She wanted his kisses never to stop.

But of course he had to stop. Jane would be waiting. And so here they are in Jane's kitchen, and all Sethie can think about are the kisses she wants to continue. The fact that those kisses are still available to her, that what they had isn't over. More kisses, more arms, more legs, all still coming. The way he can kiss her neck and her ear without tickling her. The first time Shaw ever kissed her, he first rubbed his fingers up and down her arms from behind her, where he was standing.

"That tickles," she said, giggling.

"It's not supposed to," he said, sounding irritated, and she wondered what it was supposed to do. She'd been waiting for him for months at that point, from the very start of junior year. Sethie can't remember a time when she didn't know Shaw. Their apartments are close to each other; their parents brought them to the same play groups when they were toddlers. They weren't friends, not when they were that young, and not through elementary school, when boys and girls didn't really make friends with each other.

Sethie remembers seeing Shaw at middle school dances, ridiculously outdated rituals where no one danced with anyone of the opposite sex, and in fact no one danced at all, because no one cool would ever dance at a school dance. She remembers thinking that he'd grown into a funny-looking kid, his hair a shade too dark against his pale skin, a lot of baby fat left in his face; somehow he didn't look like he had a chin. Not tall enough, a hint of acne on his cheeks.

But sometime between sophomore and junior year, Shaw grew three inches; freckles popped up all over his body, turning what had been pale skin into something colorful and interesting. His jaw became pronounced, his chin square and jutting like Clark Kent's in old *Superman* comics. And his voice changed, becoming deep and gravelly, as though over the summer he'd gotten into the habit of munching on rocks. But Sethie could never put her finger on these changes; she could never pinpoint what was new about Shaw. All she knew, and all that mattered now, was that she wanted him. She couldn't explain anything more than that; she couldn't list his fine qualities, though she knew they were abundant, and she couldn't tell you what they had in common, though she knew there was plenty; maybe she couldn't even always remember what color his eyes were, but she knew they were the most beautiful eyes she'd ever seen. And, she didn't know what it would be like if he kissed her, but she knew with certainty that Shaw must kiss her before the end of junior year. She saw him kiss other girls, out at parties, but instead of feeling jealous, she paid attention. She noticed what the other girls did before he kissed them, trying to see what it was he liked about them. And finally, one night, he was rubbing her arms so that it tickled.

He kept doing it until she understood the feeling that came after the tickles passed. Then she was grateful he hadn't stopped; she knows how close she came to sending the wrong message: I don't actually want you. Your touches make me tickle instead of tingle.

Remembering this has even distracted Sethie from the nuts. Shaw and Jane are both eating them now, and Sethie hasn't even had one.

Jane, Sethie thinks, is probably not a girl who waits for

boys to kiss her, certainly not the boy who's been kissing her for at least five months. But Jane doesn't know about Shaw's kisses. Shaw's kisses are worth waiting for. And Jane doesn't know that. Sethie is proud that Shaw chose her. Nothing else makes her this proud; not her straight As, not her 2270 on the SATs, not even the day she stepped on the scale and was under 110 pounds. All of those things are important, she knows. She worked hard for them, wanted them for a long time. And Shaw is not more important; she knows that, too. But she worked harder to get Shaw, waited longer and wanted more, to have Shaw, the boy with the beautiful cold hands, the deep voice, the eyebrows that turn blond in the sun.

"Elsa made Thanksgiving," Jane says.

"What?" Sethie asks dumbly.

"My housekeeper, Elsa, made Thanksgiving food—turkey, stuffing, mashed potatoes. Shaw, can you carve a turkey?"

Shaw shrugs. "Never tried."

"Here." Jane reaches into a drawer and brings out a knife. "Give it a try. The turkey's in the oven."

"Why did Elsa make Thanksgiving?" Sethie asks Jane. They both watch Shaw, lifting the turkey onto the stovetop, holding the knife above it, trying to decide where to begin.

"It's my favorite. Elsa always feels bad when my parents are gone too long."

Sethie wonders how long is too long. "How long have they been gone?"

"Only a week so far. But they won't be back for another week. And Thanksgiving food makes for good leftovers."

Sethie considers what would happen if there were leftover turkey, stuffing, potatoes, and pie in her kitchen. Surely she wouldn't have the discipline to make it last a whole week.

Jane starts bringing Tupperware out of the fridge.

"Wait until you try this. It's my favorite thing in the world. Ritz-cracker stuffing."

"Are you kidding?" Shaw says from the stove, where he is elbow-deep in turkey. Sethie notices that when he tries to cut the turkey, the juices at the bottom of the pan spill onto the countertop.

"I know, I know, it sounds weird. Just wait."

Sethie doesn't think it sounds weird. Sethie can barely wait. This past summer she and Shaw spent three weeks at Shaw's parents' country house. There were other kids there; Shaw's parents basically opened the house to all of his friends, but only Sethie stayed the full three weeks.

Sethie usually spends that time of year with her father. He left New York for California when Sethie was ten, after her parents split. This year, she didn't want to leave Shaw. Sethie's father didn't question it when she said she was taking an SAT prep class all summer and couldn't come. He said he was proud of her for giving up her vacation to work so hard, and Sethie almost laughed out loud. As if sitting on his couch watching TV every day was her idea of a vacation.

Three weeks with Shaw was a vacation. Sethie had to

sleep in a guest bedroom on a twin bed alongside another girl so that Shaw's parents wouldn't know they were sleeping together. When Shaw was gone during the day—he was landscaping with a local company as his summer job—and all his friends were at the beach, or sitting by the pool, or shopping in town, Sethie stayed at the house, and waited for Shaw to come home. If she went out with everyone else, she might not be there when he finished with work; he usually came home around three. When he came home, he almost always took a quick shower, and they almost always had sex before going out to meet his friends. Sethie liked it that after a few days, Shaw knew she'd be waiting for him. Having sex was the only time they were alone; Shaw's friends were waiting for him at the beach or by the pool. He couldn't spend a whole afternoon or evening with Sethie and Sethie alone; it would have been rude, and Sethie understood. Other girls sat on boys' laps at the beach, held boys' hands walking through town, kept a hand on a boy's leg under a table. Shaw didn't like public displays of affection; he told Sethie so. But Sethie could stand near him on the beach, sit next to him at dinner; Sethie wanted always to be close to him.

At the country house, while she waited for Shaw to come home from work, Sethie ate only Ritz. Shaw's parents kept the house stocked with food, and there was an enormous box of Ritz crackers in the pantry. Each day, Sethie allowed herself a maximum of six. She stretched them out over Shaw's absence. He left early, at seven-thirty. Sethie always heard him leave, but she would force herself to go back to sleep; a few more hours of sleep were a few fewer hours to be hungry. After everyone else left, she moved into Shaw's room and watched TV in his bed. Then she had two Ritz, and promised no more. Shaw would be home by three, and then they would figure out what to eat together. Surely she could make it until three with two Ritz. But then there were two more. The guilt began when she reached six and was still hungry. One day, she ate eight. She wonders, now, how many are in the stuffing. She is glad she had a small lunch.

Jane heats up gravy, Shaw carves the turkey, and Sethie just sits, watching. Jane gets out three plates, forks, and knives, puts them down on the kitchen island around which they'd been sitting on bar stools. Soon the island is covered with food. Soon they are eating. Sethie laughs at the gravy running down Shaw's face, at the jagged slices of turkey he'd cut.

Then there is pecan pie and vanilla ice cream. Sethie watches Jane eat. After a few bites of pie she leans back in her chair.

"I am so full." She puts her fork down. She stops eating.

Sethie puts her own fork down. She might be full too, but she can't be sure. Everything tastes so good.

"Should we clean up?" Shaw asks.

"No, it's okay. Elsa gets here early. I'll just put the leftovers in the fridge so they don't go bad."

Sethie knows Jane is her age, that this is her parents' house, but Jane seems like a grown-up in her own apartment.

Shaw looks at his watch. "Can I use your phone for a minute?" he says. He doesn't explain why.

"Sure," Jane says. She gestures to Sethie. "Come on, let's watch TV."

In another room—Sethie decides to call it the den—Jane sinks into a couch, turns on an enormous television.

"I am so full."

"I know," Sethie agrees, "I can't believe I ate so much." My hand will hurt, she thinks, after I finish writing down everything I've eaten.

"I know. I could barely even stop when I was full."

"I couldn't stop even then."

Jane laughs. She thinks Sethie is kidding.

Sethie says, "Sometimes I wish I could just stop eating for one week, just take a week off."

"I know what you mean," Jane says. "I tried to do one of those weeklong cleanses once, but I only lasted a day and a half."

Sethie didn't mean a cleanse. Sethie meant she wished she could just stop eating. She thinks it would actually feel better than this: What good is fullness that kicks in too late to stop her from eating too much?

"I'm so full my stomach hurts," Sethie says.

"If you really feel sick, the bathroom's right there. You could throw up."

Sethie shakes her head. "I almost never throw up. No matter how sick I feel, nothing ever happens. Not even when I try."

Jane shrugs. "I can show you, if you really want."

"What?" Sethie sits up straight, feels her stomach going out slightly, not concave under her tank top like Jane's is.

Sethie hadn't meant try like that. She meant the way you try when you don't feel well, crouching by the toilet waiting for something to happen. Not that she hasn't tried the other way. She has reached her fingers into her mouth as far as they will go, but it's never worked. The most she ever got was the occasional dry heave.

But Jane knows how to make herself throw up.

"It's really easy." Jane looks at Sethie carefully. "You sure?"

Sethie tries to stay calm. She can't let Jane see how excited she is. A solution for those nights when she overeats, when she can't stop herself.

"Yeah," she says evenly, lightly. Like she's just curious.

"Come on."

Jane leads Sethie down a hallway and into an enormous bedroom.

"This is my parents' room," she explains. "Their bathroom is perfect for this."

Sethie wonders what makes a bathroom perfect for lessons in vomiting. But then she sees. The bathroom is huge, with two toilets, each with their own door, each private. A bathroom two people can use, privately, at the same time.

"Okay, so this is the key. When you tried before, what happened?"

"Nothing. I'd gag, but nothing would come up."

"Okay, that's what you're doing wrong. You're stopping too soon. When you start to gag, keep going—keep your fingers in your mouth."

"That's all?"

"It's the easiest thing. Trust me."

Sethie turns for the bathroom. She notices Jane standing by the sinks.

"Are you going to too?"

"No, I stopped doing this in the tenth grade."

Sethie feels childish now, for needing to do this. A minute ago, it seemed exciting, illicit. Like the first time she smoked pot or the first time she and Shaw had sex. But now she feels like a baby, sloppy and fat, someone who hasn't learned to control her hunger. About to begin something she ought to have outgrown by now. Not like Jane, who stops when she's full.

"Don't do it if you don't want to, Sethie."

Sethie definitely wants to. She closes the door behind her and crouches in front of the toilet. She is pale from a summer spent mostly indoors, and her veins are visible, up and down her arms, tiny but turquoise under her skin. She doesn't notice that this floor is one solid piece of marble, so when she crouches on it, it won't leave a pattern on her bare legs. The floor of her own bathroom at home is crisscrossed with tiny tiles.

When Sethie comes out of the bathroom, Jane's back is to her; she is looking at herself in the mirror. "How'd it go?" she asks, without turning around.

"Just fine," Sethie says, like it's no big deal, trying to conceal her pride. She is so excited she wants to snap her fingers, spin in a circle, jump in the air.

"Here, use this soap."

Sethie brings her fingers to her nose. They smell. A side effect of the trick Jane has taught her: she had to keep her hand in her mouth while she was vomiting, so as she did it, her hand was covered in vomit. She wiped it off with toilet paper that stuck to her skin. Sethie thinks it's interesting that she is a lefty but she couldn't do it with her left hand. She'd had to use her right.

She must wash her face before Shaw sees her.

§ § §

In the living room, where they left the TV on, Shaw is packing a bowl.

"So where are your parents, anyway?" Sethie asks Jane as they settle beside each other on the couch.

"South America, I think."

"You think?"

"Yeah. Caracas."

"Is it for their work?"

Jane shakes her head, then reaches for the pipe. Sethie thinks she takes a hit prettily, like a girl. Sethie smokes like a boy, because Shaw is the one who taught her how.

"Not anymore," Jane says before exhaling.

"Anymore?"

"My dad's kind of semiretired. He just plays with stocks these days."

"How old is your dad?"

"Huh? No, it's not like he's retired because he's old. He was just really good at his job, so a few years ago, he quit."

"He was so good that he quit?" The logic is lost on Sethie.

"Yup. Now he just invests our money, and they travel all over."

"Sounds like fun."

Jane shrugs.

"Do you ever go with them?"

"Sometimes, over the summer. But for the last couple of years, I just kinda wanted to stay closer to home, you know?"

Sethie nods, looking over at Shaw. He's taken back the pipe, and stands up to smoke. Sethie watches the way his chest expands when he inhales and imagines her head lying against his rib cage, rising and falling with his breath.

§ § §

"You don't look like a Jane," Sethie says later, when the pot is gone and Shaw has taken control of the remote, perched on the ottoman in front of the couch where Jane and Sethie sit. Sethie means what she has said as a compliment.

"I know," Jane says. "What a dull name. Jane Virginia Scott." She wrinkles her nose. "I'll be a Daughter of the American Revolution one day."

"I'm going to call you Janey. You deserve more than one syllable."

Janey smiles. "I like that," she says.

Sethie is happy to give Janey something, even just an extra syllable, after the lesson Janey gave her tonight.

"Sethie is a cool name," Janey says, stretching her arms above her head, staring at the ceiling. "That watermark looks like a horse head," she adds.

"Where?" Sethie crosses the couch and puts her head beside Janey's, leaning against her. "There." Janey points, and then brings her arms down, around Sethie, "Can you see it?" she whispers.

"I see it now." This makes Sethie relax, lean back against her new friend. They giggle. Shaw turns around to look at them.

"What's so funny?"

"Girl stuff," Janey says possessively.

"Girl stuff," Sethie agrees.

**4.**

**S**ETHIE DOES NOT throw up again for more than a month. This is what she does do: she begins spending her afternoons at either Shaw's house or at Janey's house. Janey's parents are never home so they no longer have to go to Sethie's vacant apartment to smoke pot. Sethie does her homework alongside Janey or Shaw; Shaw helps her with calculus, and she helps Janey with her SAT words. Sethie takes the SATs a second time, even though everyone, even teachers and her mother, told her that she didn't have to since she'd done so well the first time she took them. (In fact, her score drops by ten points.) Even though it's too early to send most of them, she finishes her college applications, to ten schools, only half of which, if she is really honest with herself, she has any interest in attending. Every morning, the scale she keeps under her bed reports that she has stayed within two pounds of 111—sometimes higher, often lower—and she has been able to double-check her weight almost daily because there is an electronic scale in Janey's parents' bathroom more advanced than her computer. Sethie creates a new plan: one meal every day (usually dinner), with small snacks of pretzels, low-fat chocolate-chip granola bars, Crispix cereal, or apples with Monterey Jack cheese permitted throughout the day, but only if she gets really hungry.

She has sex with Shaw on at least four occasions each week, and each of these occasions usually includes having sex more than once. Sethie wonders how many calories all this sex burns. She goes to the gynecologist for the first time, and goes on the pill, which means that she and Shaw can stop using condoms. They were each other's first time, so it's safe. Going on the pill makes her boobs swell slightly, but so far she hasn't gained any other weight from it. And Sethie tries cocaine for the first time, one night when she and Janey and Shaw are at Janey's apartment, getting ready to go to a party at some club where someone knows the bouncer, so they won't get carded. She is frightened to try, at first, since she is prone to nosebleeds, and disgusted by the fact that they are all using the same twenty-dollar bill, which they'd chosen after some debate: using a fifty or higher was an eighties cliché, using a ten or lower was lame.

She is, actually, very disappointed with the cocaine. She doesn't feel anything. Janey and Shaw seem to like it, so she pretends to feel it too. Mostly it just makes her mouth numb, and she remembers having read somewhere that dentists used to use it on patients. Her favorite part comes after they'd snorted all they could: Shaw licks his first finger and presses it on the mirror to pick up any remains, then rubs his thumb inside Sethie's mouth, along her gums, and kisses her afterward, right in front of Janey.

"Feels different," he says, kissing her harder.

Now, Sethie is at Saks with Janey, because they've both agreed they need cooler-looking winter clothes so that they can make it through the cold weather without looking like a couple of puffballs.

"Our bodies are too good to hide under bulky sweaters and down coats," Janey announces as they enter the store, and Sethie is proud to have been thus sized up by Janey. Janey is skinny, and her skin is taut, so she must be a good judge of bodies.

"The key," Janey explains as they step off the elevator onto the fifth floor, "is tightness. We need tight jeans and tight sweaters. That way we can keep warm and look good."

"Tightness," Sethie says. The word even feels tight in her mouth, like a bra strap digging into her shoulder, elastic waistbands that leave a line on her belly, unfairly making it look like there's fat where it's really just skin pressed down too much. Tightness has never been a good thing as far as Sethie's concerned: she thinks of her school uniform, of a fat day when jeans don't fit, even though the scale says the same thing it said the day before. But Janey's tightness is altogether different, and this new kind of tightness is exciting.

"They used to say tight," Janey says, "for drunk. I think. Like Ernest Hemingway and F. Scott Fitzgerald got tight."

"Really?"

"I think so. I think that's how they meant it." Janey

shrugs. "Anyway, I like it. We should bring it back. Or invent it, if I got it wrong to begin with."

Sethie wants to be more like Janey, more like a girl who is not scared to admit she may have just invented or misunderstood an expression she heard once or twice before. Janey is very brave.

"Maybe we should give it a new meaning all its own," Sethie ventures.

"Good idea! But what will it be for?"

Sethie considers. "The perfect-fitting outfit. Like, Janey, you look tight tonight!"

Janey laughs. "Love it," she says, and heads for a table covered in jeans.

"How about these jeans?" Janey holds up a pair that look skintight even when they're folded on a shelf.

"I can't wear jeans like that," Sethie says.

"You're wrong; they're perfect. Just you wait. With your skinny legs, they'll be perfect." Janey grabs them. She doesn't ask Sethie's size, and Sethie doesn't tell her. She's curious to know what size Janey will select for her.

"Aren't you going to try them too?" Sethie asks.

"Nah, my legs aren't like yours."

The way Janey says it, Sethie knows it's a compliment. But she also notices the way Janey says it like it doesn't matter that her legs are different; she's going to find some cool clothes too, clothes that will be perfect on her own body.

And she does. Actually, Sethie finds them first: slim leather pants. She knows that they are perfect for Janey, and when she holds them up, Janey squeals. Janey doesn't look at the price tag, but Sethie looks and sees that they are 500 dollars. She hasn't looked yet at the price of the jeans that Janey picked out for her.

"Oh my God, Sethie, you have such great taste."

Sethie grins. "They're your style, not mine."

"Are you sure you don't want to try these on too?"

Sethie shakes her head. "Nope," she says. "These are all you." And she means it; she knew the minute she saw these pants that they were Janey's. But now Janey can't find her size. A saleswoman comes over when she sees Janey frantically searching the pile.

"Can I help you?"

"I hope so," Janey says, panting from her search. "I need these in a 26. Please say you have them in the back."

"We just got them in, so I'm sure I have more. I'll get you girls started in a dressing room." She takes the clothes they've gathered so far and leads them across the floor. "They're really amazing pants," she says, "very unique."

Walking behind her, Sethie and Janey exchange a smile. They are girls who know that something cannot be *very* unique, and the sound of the error is like nails on a chalkboard to them. And no matter how grateful they are, later, when the saleswoman finds the pants in Janey's size, they both believe that this separates her from them: because they know something cannot be very unique, they will never be saleswomen at Saks.

They are sharing a dressing room, of course, so that they can get each other's opinions and so that each has to show the other everything she tries on. It's a huge room, actually, with two mirrors and a bench across which they've slung their coats and bags. Janey has already slipped her pants off and is pulling the leather jeans on. Sethie thinks that she would have done the opposite; she would have waited, and tried on her favorite item last.

Sethie sits down on the bench.

"Where are your parents this week?" she asks.

"Espan-ya," Janey says, overemphasizing her accent. "Bar*the*lona, Andalu*th*ia, Ibi*th*a." Janey jumps up and down to pull the leather pants on.

"I've never been to Europe," Sethie says.

"Yeah, well." Janey turns to examine her butt in the dressing room mirror. "It's not all it's cracked up to be."

"It's not?"

Janey shrugs. "It's beautiful and all. I mean, I love the things I've seen. But"—Janey picks her hair up, as though that might help her better see how the pants fit; Sethie stares at Janey's collarbone, a straight line beneath her T-shirt—"I guess I'm just more of a homebody."

Sethie smiles. "How'd you get to be a homebody with parents who travel so much?"

"Having parents who travel so much is exactly how I became a homebody." Janey bends down to slide her pants off. "Those are definitely going in the yes pile," she says, tossing them on the floor and picking up the next pair. "I was eleven when my dad entered his semiretirement and they decided they were going to travel the world. I thought it was cool; they pulled me out of school to go to Monte Carlo. When everyone else went to camp, I was in the Swiss Alps.

But those trips weren't for me; they were for the grown-ups. You know, in Spain, no one eats dinner before ten o'clock. Do you have any idea how hard that is for a starving, jet-lagged kid who really just wants French fries and doesn't even know how to pronounce the word *paella*?"

Sethie shakes her head. "I don't. I've never been anywhere."

The girls look at each other and laugh.

"Don't worry, we'll go lots of places together," Janey says, and Sethie believes her. "Come on, I want to see those skinny jeans on you," Janey says, grabbing at the pants Sethie is holding folded in her lap.

Suddenly, Sethie is shy. She has never been undressed in front of Janey, which surprises her, though she can't imagine why it should. When would she ever have had a reason to undress in front of Janey before? This is the first time they've gone shopping together, and they're too old to have sleepovers, too young to be roommates.

Sethie is scared of what Janey will see. She is so careful to choose clothes that will cover up her flaws: the roll of fat over her belly, the hint of cellulite under her ass on her right thigh. And yet, she has worked so hard to stay close to 111 over the past few months, and she knows it looks good on her. She wants someone—a girl—to notice. Shaw only notices that she looks good, in a very general way, in whatever way it is that makes him attracted enough to her to keep sleeping with her. Shaw wouldn't understand that not many girls can wear skinny jeans, and he wouldn't know how very special it makes Sethie feel to think that she might be one of them.

So she slides out of her regular, looser jeans. She wants to pull on the new pants gracefully, sexily, but of course they get stuck around her ankles; that's how tight they are. She panics, briefly, wondering what she will do if she can't zip them in front of Janey. Janey, who is admiring herself in the mirror, turning around to see the way her butt looks in another pair of jeans.

"Not bad," she says, pursing her lips. "Let's see yours."

"They might be too tight," Sethie says. Janey picked out a size 27 for Sethie; one size larger, Sethie knows, than what Janey herself wears.

"You haven't even pulled them up yet," Janey points out, and it's true. The pants are still below Sethie's hips, because she's too scared to pull them any higher.

"Want me to help?" Janey offers. Sethie nods.

Janey steps away from the mirror, stands behind Sethie, very close, and puts her hands on either side of her, then grips the jeans. She slides them up over Sethie's hips, and then Sethie steps away from her to zip and button them.

"Sethie, are you crazy? These fit you perfectly."

Sethie has never worn anything so tight.

"Are you sure?"

"Yes, nut job. They're supposed to be tight. All of your clothes are too big."

"They are?"

Janey shrugs. "Sometimes. You know, wearing things

loose makes you look fatter, not thinner," Janey says matter-of-factly.

Sethie looks at herself in the mirror. Janey is right. Her legs look skinnier in these tight jeans than in the looser ones she'd been wearing earlier. And she deserves that, she thinks. All that work, and the only person who sees it is Shaw, when she's naked, and that's usually only under covers.

"You'll wear them tonight."

"What's tonight?"

"Didn't Shaw tell you?"

Sethie shakes her head. They always do something on Saturday nights, but Sethie doesn't usually find out what ahead of time. Shaw's not a planner.

"There's a party up at Columbia. Jeff Cooper—do you know him?" Sethie nods. "He graduated last year. He invited us, since Shaw wants to go to school there."

Jeff Cooper went to their school, Shaw and Janey's: Houseman.

"Shaw will love that," Sethie says, feeling possessive. "That's actually what he's doing today, right now. Working on his Columbia application."

Sethie has known that Shaw wants to go to Columbia forever. Certainly longer than Janey has known it. She has no idea why she feels threatened. She wishes it would go away.

"Yeah, pretty cool. Anyway, Shaw's bringing a bunch of us. It'll be fun. Like, a frat party, how cheesy is that?"

"Pretty cliché."

"Well, no getting drunk and losing your virginity to some frat brother. That's a little too Lifetime Television for Women."

Janey must be joking, Sethie thinks. Janey must know that Sethie wouldn't disappear with anyone, because she will be there with Shaw tonight. She must know that Sethie and Shaw have been sleeping together for months and months.

"That would be impossible, Janey, but I'll be sure to keep an eye on *you*." Sethie pretends it's a joke, but she knows she's only saying it to point something out.

Janey laughs.

"Well then," she says, "I guess both of us are in the clear."

Sethie pays with cash; her mother gave it to her before she left the house this morning, though Sethie thinks she probably assumed it wouldn't all be spent on one pair of jeans. Rebecca has promised to get her a credit card next year, when she needs it to buy books and food at college. Janey pays with a gray American Express that Sethie knows is not really gray but platinum, and she explains that her parents have black ones. Until then, Sethie didn't know that they came in black.

They walk back uptown. In the dressing room, Janey made it clear that she is not a virgin either. Janey may know many things, but she doesn't know about the tuft of hair that began to grow on Shaw's chest after his birthday this year, or the way he closed his eyes when he touched Sethie's breasts for the first time, and certainly Janey doesn't know that his mouth is always cool, his tongue always soft but ice-cold.

Sethie knows these things should be private, but she wants to tell. She wants to tell Janey about sex with Shaw. It's like the skinny jeans that, having seen on her body, she suddenly found herself wanting. Wanting to show off something she worked hard to get, something she thinks too much about, something she wanted so badly: skinny legs.

**T HOME, SETHIE** closes her bedroom door, even though her mother is out. She takes off all of her clothes except her underwear and puts the jeans on. Sethie knows that dressing room mirrors sometimes lie; maybe these won't look the same out in the world. She's only just gotten home; her hair is still cool from the weather outside, but she's already thinking that she should probably return these pants. She didn't take off her shirt in the dressing room because she didn't want Janey to see her belly fat. But now, without a shirt on, she can see the way her belly fat bunches up around the waistline. She pulls out her desk chair and plants it in front of the full-length mirror on the back of her door. The fat is much worse when she sits down.

She stands again, turning her back to the mirror and twisting her neck. From behind, the jeans do look pretty good. Maybe they're so tight that they're holding her ass in, molding it into shape the way it should be. And she also knows her ass is pretty thin this week. She knows because on Tuesday, they had an assembly at school, and when Sethie sat cross-legged on the floor in the assembly room, she could feel her bones against the hardwood.

It was an emergency assembly; the prior week's *New York* magazine cover story had been called "Sex and the High School Girl," and it claimed that girls from New York City's elite all-girls private schools were having way more sex than their parents and teachers realized. Like maybe that was the result of single-sex education, because none of the girls from the coed "elite private schools" were mentioned. Sethie thought it was odd that the article—which all the girls read; there was even a copy circulating in the senior lounge—didn't acknowledge that that must mean that the private-school boys were having more sex, too; otherwise who were these girls all having their inordinate amounts of sex with? But the article didn't seem to think that was the problem; or in any case, it wasn't the story.

The article was based on interviews with girls from these "elite private schools," but it didn't say which schools the girls who'd been interviewed attended. Everyone knows which schools the article meant, though. There are three pretty competitive all-girls schools in the city, and of course Sethie's school, the White School, is one of them. There's an old joke—Sethie assumes that it's old; everyone seems to know it, and she can't remember when she first heard it—that the girls at one school will grow up to marry the lawyers, the girls from another will grow up to become the lawyers, and the girls from the third will grow up to sleep with the lawyers. Which girls do which tends to switch based on which school the girl who's telling the joke attends, but Sethie notices that no one ever says that theirs is the school from which the girls marry the lawyers. Anyway, Sethie thinks lawyers are out of fashion nowadays. It should be, she thinks, bankers, or maybe dot-com geniuses, or whatever they call those guys who make millions off the Internet. But no, Sethie decides, the Internet isn't really a New York thing. Well, they should add bankers, in any case.

Sethie sat during the assembly, watching the head-mistress squirm as she alluded to a "certain item" in the article. The certain item she couldn't bring herself to describe was the story in which one of the girls interviewed told the reporter about a party where all the girls offered to give the boys blow jobs as, say, the cover charge to get in. Everyone at White knows it's not true; everyone at all the private schools knows that never happened. It was just a story; it was just a punch line. Sethie thinks that the un-named source probably didn't think the reporter would even believe it; Sethie can't imagine that anyone she knows would have believed it.

A girl in Sethie's class claims to know the girl who told the story. Actually, she says, it was three girls, and they all go to the school around the corner, the school every-one knows isn't quite as academically rigorous as White is. They thought it would be cool to be in a magazine, but then they lost their nerve and asked to be quoted anonymously. Sethie wonders if it's even legal to quote girls under the age of eighteen and use their names without their parents' permission.

Sethie sat on the floor of the assembly room, even though the seniors are allowed to sit in the chairs in the back that are otherwise reserved for faculty use only. The headmistress talked about the dangers of speaking to reporters, the importance of preserving White's 100-year-old reputation. When she asked if anyone had any questions, Sethie was tempted to ask why the headmistress (who apparently believed the story) was more concerned with the girls speaking to reporters than she was with girls giving blow jobs to get into a party. Sethie leaned against the wall near the door. Cross-legged, she could feel three sets of bones in this position: the bones beneath her ass, her ankles, and her shoulder blades. Sethie imagines that being really fat must be like having a constant cushion; there must be no hard surfaces, Sethie thinks, for the obese.

Now, Sethie stares at her butt in the mirror, at the stitching over the pockets in the denim. These pants remind her of how she used to dress, years ago, when she was thirteen and fourteen and her mother still helped her pick out her clothes, just like she had when she was a little girl, even though her body had defiantly stopped being a little girl's. Sethie's breasts came late, but now they are here to stay; no matter how much weight she loses, she always needs to wear a bra. Her mother came into dressing rooms with her then; now, if they do shop together, Sethie never lets her in. Rebecca told her how clothes should fit, and Rebecca—skinny, small Rebecca—said that clothes should be tight, so her daughter wore them tight. Now, Sethie can hardly believe she walked around like that. She remembers her short shorts and the way men began to stare at her. She liked it at first; it made her feel pretty. It even made her feel stylish, as though her clothes were what they noticed, not her body underneath them. And it made her feel grown-up, old enough for adult men to notice.

Once, in ninth grade, she was meeting someone at the Met, and she got there early. She was wearing an army green short skirt and a white tank top. An outfit her mother loved so much that they both tried it on in the dressing room, and Rebecca had insisted that they share it, since they could only afford to buy one set. Sethie was already two inches taller than her mother, so the skirt wasn't nearly as short on Rebecca, something Rebecca didn't seem to notice; or if she did, she didn't think it was a problem.

Sethie sat on the steps of the Met and waited for her classmate. It was the end of the school year, and their ancient-history teacher had assigned them all a trip to the Greek wing of the Met as their final project. They each had to pick an artifact to write about, and they were supposed to go to the museum in pairs. The school said it was for safety.

There was a man on a bicycle at the bottom of the steps, and he stared at Sethie. At first, she liked it. She pretended not to notice; she pretended to be oblivious. She played with her hair and chewed on her pen, pretending to make notes in her notebook. When she looked up, she saw that the man hadn't moved at all; he was staring right at her, smiling. Sethie hadn't intended to make eye contact, but she had. She was surprised when he didn't look away; most men looked away once they saw that she could tell they were watching her. They usually seemed ashamed, or embarrassed. But this man went right on staring.

Sethie stood up. She stuffed her notebook into her backpack (she still used a backpack then), and walked to the other side of the steps. The steps are enormous, she remembers thinking, surely he won't be so shameless as to follow me to the other side. She thought he would lose sight of her among all the other people milling around and sitting on the steps. But he rode his bicycle from one side of the steps to the other, keeping his eyes on her, on her bare arms and bare legs, on the tiny stripe of stomach that peeked out from under her tank top when she moved.

When she got home that night, she took off the skirt and the tank top and told Rebecca she could keep them. They don't really fit me, Sethie explained. I'm bigger than you, Sethie said, we can't really share clothes anymore. Rebecca had shrugged. Sethie thinks she was probably pretty happy to have the outfit to herself.

Sethie puts on a shirt. With a loose shirt on, she can barely see the roll of fat at the top of her new jeans, and the bottom half really does look good; Janey was right. Sethie decides she will keep the pants; she will wear them tonight at least, even if she hides them in the back of her closet after that, even if they will become her "skinny jeans," the jeans she tries on only in her room to gauge whether she is having a fat week or a thin week. But she will wear them tonight; Janey would be disappointed if she didn't.

**JANEY HAS INVITED** everyone to meet at her apartment before heading up to Columbia. First, Shaw picks Sethie up. He's wearing jeans with a Polo T-shirt, which he has tucked in, and a belt that looks strange to Sethie, though she's not sure exactly what's wrong with it. Sethie would never say it out loud, but she knows that Shaw does not dress well. He buys the right clothes, but he wears them all wrong. That shirt should not be tucked in. He should not be wearing white socks with those sneakers. And something about the belt needs fixing.

Sethie is wearing her new jeans with a black tank top layered under a cardigan and scarf, black boots with high heels. She's wearing makeup, which she doesn't wear often: brown eyeliner and mascara, blush and lip gloss. She doesn't think she's ever looked so good for Shaw, and she's proud when she opens the door. Sethie is excited for the party; excited to be Shaw's girl, looking good, at a party.

Excited to get a sneak peek at Columbia; Sethie wants to go there too. Excited because she always has fun when she's with Janey.

Shaw kisses her hello. "Your lips are sticky," he says, and rubs his own lips, to wipe away any trace of gloss from having kissed her. He hasn't had a chance to take in the whole outfit yet, Sethie thinks. He'll see that her lips need to be sticky when he sees how good the gloss looks.

Sethie turns her back to him, steps into the apartment so he can see her. She picks up her purse from the dining room table, turns around to face him, her arm leaning on the back of a chair, her hip cocked. She is posing.

"You look nice," Shaw says finally.

Sethie smiles. "Thanks." She grabs her coat from the back of the chair she'd been leaning on. "You too," she adds, even though she knows she's lying. Shaw's handsome, but he doesn't look particularly great now, in his clothes that aren't right at all.

It's okay, Sethie thinks. She looks right enough for the both of them. Shaw says they should walk to Janey's building. It's only ten blocks. Sethie is freezing, but she agrees. She didn't think they'd be outside much tonight; Janey said they'd take a cab up to Columbia. So Sethie had decided to wear a light coat; her warmer one isn't nearly stylish enough.

"Why aren't you wearing gloves?" Shaw asks after a few blocks of walking side by side.

"You're not."

"But the cold doesn't bother me like you."

Like it bothers you, Sethie thinks, correcting his grammar in her head.

"I don't like gloves."

"Come here," he says, putting his arm around her. "You can put your hands in my pocket."

Now Sethie is very happy they have decided to walk to Janey's instead of taking a cab. Walking, Shaw is holding her close. She could never tell him that he doesn't actually keep her warm, that it would be easier, and warmer, to keep her hands in her own pockets, and really it would help more if he would just carry her purse for her. She would never say that; she would prefer to be cold because his arms feel so good around her. He wants to make her warm, and that makes Sethie happy.

After walking in the cold, the heat in Janey's apartment hurts. Sethie's fingers feel like they're burning, and she goes straight to the bathroom and runs water over them, starting with cold water and warming it up slowly, until her hands feel normal again. Shaw joins the group in the living room: Janey, and two other guys who must have known Jeff Cooper too.

In the bathroom, Sethie looks at her face in the mirror above the sink. The wind wore off her lip gloss, but her cheeks are pink and glowing. Her eyes are red, but they look very bright and shiny. Sethie reapplies her lip gloss and wipes her nose. She opens and closes her hands a few times. She wonders how late they will be out tonight. She's told her mother she'll be staying at Janey's.

When she emerges from the bathroom, Janey is fixing Shaw's shirt.

"A shirt like this should not be tucked in, buddy," she says. Her blond hair is pulled into a tight ponytail. Sethie thinks Janey's cheekbones look expensive. Cheekbones like Janey's are exactly the kind a plastic surgeon would give you.

"All right, all right, thanks, Janey," Shaw says. Shaw doesn't blush, and he doesn't seem embarrassed or even bothered that Janey is fixing him and touching him. Sethie always waits for Shaw to touch her first. It's only polite, she thinks, since she knows she always wants him touching her, but can't be sure when he wants her touching him.

"Wait, something else," Janey says, reaching for Shaw as he is about to step away, maybe toward Sethie.

"Your belt," she says, grabbing for it, shifting it to the side like it should be. Easily identifying what had been wrong with it. Sethie inhales; her throat is tight, her skin itches. Janey's fingers fold over Shaw's waistband carelessly, without any sense of the intimacy of it. Sethie isn't sure whether she's jealous that Janey is touching Shaw's waist, or that Janey was able to identify what was wrong and fix it so easily.

"There," Janey says, satisfied, mussing up Shaw's hair as though for good measure. Then she turns to Sethie. "Honestly, how can you let him out of the house like this?" A question that Sethie understands is Janey's way of giving Shaw back to her, having taken him for just a second. And a gesture for which Sethie is grateful, since it makes clear to everyone that Shaw belongs to her. That even though Janey fixed him, really she was just doing it on Sethie's behalf.

Janey walks over to Sethie now. Sethie wonders if she's about to be fixed, too.

"You look fantastic," Janey announces. Sethie blushes. "Those jeans are perfect," she says, and Sethie is grateful for this. Warm now, she's become very aware of the denim on her legs—literally touching her legs. She's used to feeling some air between her body and the cloth of her clothes, every touch of that air confirmation that she is thin. These jeans definitely don't allow for air. Janey says clothes should be tight, not loose. Maybe she thinks that Sethie used to be heavier, and that's why all her clothes are too big. She might not know that Sethie buys them that way because she likes the way loose clothes feel. And certainly, Janey doesn't know how it feels when you do gain weight, when your clothes become the other kind of tight, too tight, grabbing onto your fat like grubby, angry hands. Sethie needs to buy her clothes loose because she needs the insurance for when she does gain weight, as she is always frightened she will.

Everyone is drinking Janey's parents' booze. Top-shelf, Sethie thinks, though she's not entirely sure what it means. They're all buzzed by the time they leave the apartment. The cabdriver groans when he sees that there are five of them; four is the limit, he insists.

"We'll give you a big tip," Janey promises, and the cabdriver waves them into the backseat.

Sethie sits on Shaw's lap. Janey sits in front with the driver. No one ever wants to get stuck sitting up front with the driver, and Sethie is disappointed none of the boys volunteered in Janey's place. They all piled in. Even Shaw didn't wait for Sethie to go in first. Sethie wonders if boys raised in other places—places where there isn't such an emphasis on rushing, where you don't have to scramble for a seat or be left standing, gripping a pole on the subway— have better manners, or if chivalry really is dead, everywhere. But then, she thinks, sitting up front with the cab driver would be a very New York–specific kind of chivalry.

Shaw's hands rest on her waist; he slips two fingers under her waistband. Shaw's fingers are so cold that Sethie inhales sharply, but then she is grateful for the reflex, because now she's sucking in her belly.

The frat house isn't like the houses in movies. It's a tall, skinny town house just like the ones on side streets on the Upper East Side—not as nice as the ones closer to Fifth, but no more run-down or beat-up than some of the ones farther east, near Second Avenue. The boys go in first, and Janey and Sethie hold hands and follow. Janey's fingertips poke through her gloves.

"Cut the tips off," she explains when she sees Sethie looking. "That way I can smoke without taking them off."

"Very cool," Sethie says, and Janey grins.

It's stuffy inside the house; almost immediately Sethie is aware of sweat forming on her upper lip. There's no place to put their coats; it looks like everyone else lives so close by that they didn't bother wearing coats for the walk over. Sethie unwinds her scarf, unbuttons her jacket, but she can't imagine just leaving them somewhere here. The floors feel sticky; the sofas look grimy. Maybe she can just keep them on. Maybe they won't be here that long, or maybe she'll get used to the heat. She can fit her clutch into one of the pockets. She notices that none of the girls here are carrying purses.

"Come on," Janey says, pulling Sethie toward the stairs. The boys have walked beyond them already, into the party, and presumably closer to the booze.

"Wait, are we supposed to go up there?"

"I don't know, but we've got to find a decent place to put our coats, right?"

They walk up one flight, then another. The higher they get, the less grimy it looks.

"I guess the more important people live up higher," Janey says. Sethie shrugs. On the third floor, they see a boy coming out of a room, closing the door behind him.

"Hey!" Janey says.

"Yeah?"

"That your room?"

"Yeah," he says, raising his eyebrows.

"Is it clean?"

"What?" he says, laughing. Sethie guesses he must be at least a sophomore.

"Is your room clean?"

"Why?"

"Look, dude, it's a yes-or-no question."

He laughs. Sethie wonders if he can tell they're in high school, or maybe he thinks they're cocky freshmen. She's happy to let Janey do the talking.

"It's not."

"It's dirty?"

"No, it's not a yes-or-no question. It's too strange to be a yes-or-no question."

Janey opens her mouth, but nothing comes out. Sethie's never seen her stumped for a good rejoinder, and even the boy she's been talking to seems to know that he's done something unusual—stumped the strange girl with the bright lipstick, even though no one wears that kind of lipstick these days.

He throws Janey a rope. "It's clean. I'm a chemistry major."

Janey still doesn't say anything, so Sethie speaks. "What does being a chemistry major have to do with having a clean room?"

Janey grins like she's proud of Sethie for asking the question. Later, she'll tell Sethie: "I love when you're a smart-ass."

The boy says, "Dunno. Just seems like it does, I guess."

"Can we use your room?" Sethie asks.

He raises his eyebrows again. "What for?"

Janey seems to come back down to earth. "Don't be a perv. For our coats."

"People are stacking their coats on the couch in the basement, I think."

Janey wrinkles her nose. "Gross. We're not leaving our coats down there. Who knows what'll end up getting done on top of them?"

He laughs.

"Good point. Use the room." He opens the door behind him; Sethie notices then that he'd never actually taken his hand off the doorknob.

He stands against the door so they have to squeeze past him to get inside. Sethie goes first.

"What's your name?" Janey asks when it's her turn.

"Doug."

"You're supposed to ask for our names now," Janey says, entering the room, slipping her coat off her shoulders, unwinding her scarf. When Janey's scarf is completely unwound, she slides out of her cardigan, revealing her scoop-neck top. Sethie notices a sheen of sweat over her collarbone; it looks like Janey's clavicle is glowing.

Sethie grabs Janey's coat, puts it over her arm with her own.

"Where should I put these?"

"Over there." Doug points to his desk. Sethie lays the coats over the back of his chair. He's holding his keys. Sethie's worried that when they want to leave, they'll have to find Doug to let them back in here, to get their coats. Sethie is worried they won't be able to find him, or maybe he'll be back in here, asleep, and they'll have to wake him for their coats. These kinds of concerns never seem to occur to anyone else.

Janey is still standing in the center of the room, waiting for Doug to ask their names. Sethie doesn't think he's going to.

"I'm Sethie," she says finally. "This is Jane."

"Nice to meet you," Doug says.

"You too. Thanks for the room." She looks at Janey. "Want to go find the boys?" Sethie asks deliberately. She feels like they've been in this room, with this strange boy, for a long time. She wants him to know they didn't come alone.

Janey shrugs. "I guess." Sethie steps toward the door. "Wait," Janey says. "Are you locking the door?"

"Yes. Of course."

"Then how will we get our coats when we're ready to leave?" Sethie almost grins because Janey's thought of the same problem she has. But when Doug responds, she realizes that Janey wasn't worried about the coats at all.

"Guess you'll just have to stick with me all night, then." He cocks his head toward the hall. "Come on."

Both girls squeeze past Doug again and wait while he locks the door behind him. Sethie sees that Janey's clavicle is glowing even harder now.

# 7.

**SHAW'S FINGERS ARE** long and thin, like a piano player's fingers, and Sethie recognizes them when the only part of him that she can see with all the people between them are his fingers wrapped around a beer can. Sethie and Janey are sitting on a couch by the front door with Doug, and Shaw is across the room, close to the kitchen, close to a tub filled with beer and ice. Doug has gotten them "real" drinks, some pinkish substance that Sethie can only guess is very cheap vodka mixed with Kool-Aid powder or maybe Crystal Light. She hopes it's Crystal Light: fewer calories.

"There's Jeff Cooper," she says to Janey, even though what she really means is There's Shaw, standing next to Jeff Cooper, talking to him, and I think we should go over there. I'd like to go over there. But she won't get up: tonight is for Shaw to see what a cool girlfriend she is. The kind who doesn't hang on you at a party; the kind you can nod to from across the room and not have to check up on.

"Oh," Janey says absently.

Sethie is hot. She should have left her sweater in Doug's room too, with her coat, the way Janey did with hers. There are so many people crunched into this space that even the booze is lukewarm. Sethie thinks of what they normally drink, back on the east side of town; it's better than this. But it's all the same: it's still something you try to swallow without tasting.

Sethie knows how she looks when she gets hot like this. Her hair falls flat and her skin gets blotchy. Sweating under her tight jeans, she is very aware of the denim against her skin, and she can't for the life of her remember what she was thinking, buying these pants. She is not a skinny-jeans girl. Skinny-jeans girls are taller than she is, and lankier. They are flat-chested and don't need to wear bras. Sethie knows no matter how much weight she loses, she'll never be that kind of girl.

The heat doesn't seem to bother Janey. Her skin is dewy with sweat. Her blond hair was already greasy and messy in a ponytail, so a little sweat doesn't ruin it. She didn't blow it dry and try to make it fluffy like Sethie did a few hours ago. And Janey, Sethie realizes, is Lanky. Lanky isn't bothered by the heat, and Lanky doesn't have sweat building up underneath her breasts, because Lanky is flat-chested.

Janey is laughing at everything Doug says. For a while, Sethie was trying to listen too, trying to get the joke, but it's so loud, and nothing he said seemed that funny, so after a while she gave up the effort of listening. She was sure Shaw would have come to find her by now. But he seems perfectly content, across the room, hands on his beer, talking to the boys. Sethie can wait; she is determined to be the cool, independent girl that Shaw will come find, not the other way around. So she sits squeezed between the arm of the couch and Janey, with Doug on Janey's other side, and waits. Sethie wonders how it's possible for Janey to be at least an inch taller than she is and yet seem so much smaller. She tries to keep smiling, so that when Shaw looks over, he'll see what a cool, independent girl she is, and he'll be happy that she's his.

"Doug's getting us more drinks," Janey says suddenly. Sethie hadn't even noticed he'd gotten up.

"Oh?"

"Yes. I told him we wanted beers now."

"Okay."

"He's really cute."

"Really?" Sethie corrects herself. "Really." Sethie doesn't think he's that cute.

"It's not like normal colleges, you know. I mean, we live here."

"What?"

"I mean, it's not like having a high school girlfriend back home. I just live across town."

Sethie wonders when Janey became Doug's girlfriend.

"You guys can go back without me. The doorman will let you in, no problem."

"Wait, what are you talking about? You want us to leave you here?" Sethie shifts her weight on the couch. She thinks if the room was quieter, she would be able to hear the denim groaning against her thighs. "I'm not going to leave you here. We don't know anything about Doug. We shouldn't even be drinking the drinks he gave us."

"Why not?"

"We didn't see them get made or get poured. Who knows what we've been drinking?"

"Oh my God, Sethie, lighten up. They're just normal drinks."

"They don't taste good."

Janey shrugs.

"I'm gonna go tell the boys." Janey gets up. Sethie does not want to be left on this couch alone, waiting.

"Tell them what?"

"Just stay here for a second."

Sethie fights the urge to follow Janey when she walks away. She knows Janey wants her to stay in case Doug comes back. She hates this kind of music. It's hip-hop, that much she can recognize. She wants to point out the fact that there is not a single black person in the room, and all these white people look ridiculous singing along like they can relate to Tupac.

"Hey," Doug says, sitting down next to her, holding three cans of beer. Sethie notices that they're closed. "Where'd Janey go?"

"To talk to our friends, I think." Sethie wonders when Doug started calling her Janey, too.

"Oh. Here." He hands one of the beers to Sethie. She doesn't open it. No point wasting the calories if she's about to leave.

"Janey said you went to a different school."

"What?"

"Janey said you and she don't go to the same school."

"No. Mine's all girls." Sethie looks across the room, watching for Janey coming back to them, trying to see Shaw.

"What's that like?"

"I've never gone to anything but an all-girls school, so I'm used to it."

"There's an all-girls part of Columbia."

"I know. I'm applying there."

"So I guess you like the all-girls thing, huh?"

Sethie turns and looks straight at Doug. For some reason what he's said seems offensive to her. Like he thinks he knows more about her than he possibly could.

"Well, it hasn't seemed to keep me from meeting boys anyway."

Doug laughs, his teeth looking very white in the dark room. Sethie thinks that if there was a black light, his teeth would glow.

"Hey." Sethie and Doug turn away from each other, look up to see Janey standing in front of them.

"The boys are waiting outside for you," she says to Sethie. "I went up and got your coat." She holds it out.

Sethie wonders when Janey got Doug's keys from him. She wonders exactly when she became the third wheel on their first date; was it the minute he opened the door to his room? Sethie knows she's supposed to stand up, take her coat, and leave. It feels strange just leaving Janey like this, going back to Janey's house without her. But Janey's looking at her expectantly, so Sethie stands.

"It was nice meeting you, Doug," she says, taking her coat. Doug stands up to say good-bye to her, and Sethie thinks maybe he's nicer than she's given him credit for. "I'll see you later," she adds to Janey, more a plea than a good-bye.

"Later," Janey says, sitting back down on the couch with Doug. Sethie wonders how many minutes they will wait before they start making out, once she's gone. She wonders whether they will start on this couch or go up to Doug's room. She wonders whether Doug's frat brothers will make fun of him in the morning, for hooking up with a high school girl, or give him triumphant high fives for achieving the feat in such a short amount of time.

At first, the outside air feels amazing against her hot skin, and Sethie feels perked up. But then the cold snakes its way to all the places where she'd been sweating, and her teeth begin to chatter.

"Dude, where have you been?" Shaw calls to her. He's standing on the corner. "I had to let the guys go in a cab. Janey said you'd be right out."

Sethie is confused. Has she done something wrong? She was only just given her coat; she only hesitated a second before leaving. She notices the boys didn't seem to have any qualms about leaving Janey at the party. Maybe Jeff Cooper knows Doug. Maybe he told them all that he was a nice guy.

"Does Jeff Cooper know Doug well?" she asks Shaw, once they're settled into a cab.

"Huh?"

"The guy Janey and I hung out with. Does Jeff know him?"

"I don't know," Shaw says irritably. "I guess. I mean, they're in the same fraternity."

"Okay." Sethie wonders why Shaw seems like he's in such a bad mood.

"Did you have fun?" she asks carefully.

"I was."

"Huh?" she says dumbly.

"Dude, I was having fun. But you spend the whole night talking to some random guy, and then you tell Janey to come get me because you want to come home?"

"What?"

"Look, Janey wasn't going to lie and pretend she wanted to go home too. So I had to take you."

"I never . . . I didn't say that."

"I didn't want to leave yet."

"I'm sorry," Sethie says, not entirely sure why this is her fault. But she's also a little excited, because it sounds like Shaw was actually jealous that she spent the evening talking to Doug. But then, why didn't he come get her? She spent the whole night purposely not hanging out with him, purposely giving him space. She thinks she's completely bungled being the cool girlfriend she wanted to be.

"I'm sorry," Sethie says again, and she really does feel sorry. She wishes she'd done better.

"Let's get some food," Shaw says, and instructs the cab-driver to let them out on Lexington, a couple of blocks away from Janey's house, where there's a pizza place that's open late. Sethie doesn't want to eat, but she doesn't want Shaw to be angry at her. So she eats the pizza he puts in front of her, the whole thing, except the crust, she never eats the crust, and she thinks Shaw knows that, so surely he won't be angry at her for not eating everything he's given her.

Janey's doorman lets them up without asking for an explanation: maybe Janey told him to expect them without her. In the elevator, Shaw begins to kiss her and Sethie sinks against the wall, bending her knees toward each other to touch so that she won't lose her balance. Shaw is taller than she is and he bends over Sethie so that she has to lean her neck back far, until it feels like the back of her head is between her shoulder blades. When he runs his hands down her body, she can feel how cold they are through her jeans. When she shivers, her jeans don't feel so tight. Shaw holds her arms on either side, and Sethie thinks that if he squeezed just a little bit harder, his fingers might go right through her, as if her flesh and bone were nothing more than a piece of thick cake.

"Come on," he says softly, leading her by the hand (does this count as hand-holding, she wonders) toward Janey's parents' bedroom. Sethie doesn't hesitate at the door, just follows him. As he lays her back on the bed, she stares at the ceiling wondering whether Janey's parents would mind, and whether Janey would mind, whether this was the room Janey had in mind when she said they could stay over.

She doesn't want to be a girl who thinks like that when a boy like this is kissing her. She wants instead to concentrate on Shaw, pushing her shirt under her armpits, kissing her belly and making her, just for a second, glad for the softness there, for the way it feels when he presses against it; right now, it just feels like soft, not like fat.

And so she thinks about his kisses, and his hands giving her goose bumps, and when it's over she gets up to go to the bathroom, and only then does she turn the light on, and only then does she see her nakedness in the light, and she remembers the first time she was in this bathroom, and what she did here. Looking at herself in the full-length mirror next to the sinks, she runs her hands over her rib cage. She isn't skinny enough to count her bones there, the way she's heard some anorexics do, and she can see how counting the bones would be comforting, a reminder of where your efforts to lose weight must end: bones that jut out defiantly, saying *You cannot get any thinner than we are.* Sethie pinches the skin over her ribs. She could still be thinner.

It doesn't count, she thinks, as she leans over the toilet. I was drinking so much, so really, it's just so I won't have a hangover in the morning. And I didn't even want that pizza, I didn't need it, so it's not fair that I should have to have those calories in me.

Even though she's only done it once before, and months ago, she knows she must do it quickly, before Shaw notices she's been gone very long. She limits herself to just two tries. She is delighted when soon she sees the pink of the drink she had at the beginning of the night. That's hours' worth of calories.

Shaw falls asleep first, which doesn't surprise Sethie. His arms are around her, but she's cold so she disentangles herself, moves over toward the edge of the enormous bed, deeper under the covers, so that they are around her head like a hood, with only her face peeking out. She doesn't mind not being able to sleep; she hadn't expected to be able to sleep. She doesn't mind watching the walls, and the way that the pattern on the wallpaper kind of looks like thorns, even though it's just supposed to be vines. Janey's parents have expensive taste, it's clear to her, even in the dark. She wonders how much goose down is packed into this comforter; what a waste it would be to fall asleep when the bed feels this good: the sheets crisp and clean but warm; the pillows so thick that they bounce back into shape when you lift your head.

This, Sethie thinks, is a big grown-ups' bed in a big grown-ups' house. Shaw and I would never have a place like this, we'd never need all this. Sethie is embarrassed to have even had that thought. That was ridiculous. I know better than to plan a future with my high school boyfriend. I even know better than to call him my boyfriend. No one uses words like that anymore.

Well, some people, she thinks. One of Shaw's friends has a long-distance girlfriend, and he never comes out with them, and never comes over to smoke; he's too busy calling his girlfriend. And that annoying girl in her physics class, she has a "boyfriend," and they're even talking about going to the same college, even though everyone knows that's a mistake. Girls aren't supposed to choose schools based on where their boyfriends go. No girl stays with her high school boyfriend once she gets to college. There are always breakups. Sethie knows that she and Shaw will become just friends once it's time to leave for school next year, since they might go to different places. They were really just friends before they got together, so it should be easy to do. Still, she can't really picture it, can't quite imagine it. So lately she doesn't think about the future much. She got her college applications done early, so it's all out of her hands now; she doesn't have to think about it at all. She just has to lie in this bed with Shaw, cozy under these grown-up covers, careful not to wake him up.

Sethie likes finishing things early, though she wonders whether her applications will be on the bottom of the admissions pile, just by virtue of having arrived at each of the colleges so early. One college asked her to write about her greatest achievement for her essay. She actually began writing an essay about staying under 111 pounds; she wrote about how good her hip bones felt on the floor when she did her daily leg lifts, about how carefully she sipped her coffee and spread her peanut butter. She would never have used the essay. At White, you have to go over your admissions essays with the college advisor before submitting them, and an essay like that would have set off alarms throughout the school. They'd have told her mother; they'd have sent her to therapy. Clearly, weight loss was not an appropriate achievement, even if it was the most honest one. So Sethie wrote about last year's yearbook production, back when she used to go to meetings, back when she actually thought that mattered more than how much she weighed.

At five a.m. (Sethie had been watching the time on the digital clock on her side of the bed, which she assumes must be Janey's father's side, since the clock on the other side of the bed is prettier and old-fashioned-looking), Sethie hears footsteps. High heels on the marble in the entranceway, she thinks: Janey's home.

Janey stops outside her parents' room and opens the door. From the bed, Sethie can see her outline, silvery with the light from the hallway behind her, and Sethie knows she is supposed to get up and follow Janey to her room, to talk with her about Doug. Sethie keeps the covers around her while she looks for Shaw's Polo shirt and boxers to slip on. Shaw is so much bigger than she is that the waistband of his boxers is loose around her belly, and Sethie feels deliciously thin as she slips out of bed.

Janey doesn't turn the lights on in her room. She opens her window and props herself on the sill, lights a cigarette, and offers one to Sethie. There's only a little light coming in from outside, but Sethie can imagine that Janey's collarbone is still aglow. She lights a cigarette too, exhales the smoke out the window, looks down onto Park Avenue. It's a moment before she looks over and notices Janey's teeth, bright in the light coming in from the street, just like Doug's at the party. Janey is smiling widely: even when she brings her cigarette to her lips, the smile stays.

**S**ETHIE WAKES UP before Shaw. She lies still in the bed, listening to his breathing. With the shades drawn, it's still dark, even though it's nearly eleven. She really should, she knows, go home. Even though she's just woken up, the day is nearly half over. She has an English paper to finish, and French homework to do. She wishes she'd brought some work with her here to Janey's; that way she could get it done while Shaw and Janey sleep. When she was a little kid, she was always the first to wake up at sleepover parties. She always packed a book along with her sleeping bag, and she remembers finishing countless Baby-sitters Clubs and Boxcar Childrens while everyone else slept. She doesn't even consider waking Shaw, since she knows, from having stayed with him this summer, how angry he gets when he's woken up against his will. A girl in her class told Sethie how she once woke a boy up by giving him a blow job. Sethie doesn't think that's the kind of thing that would go over with Shaw.

Shaw's back is to her anyway; he's curled almost into the fetal position. Sethie slides to the edge of the bed and tiptoes to the bathroom. She closes the door and turns on the light. Her eyes are bright red; it looks like she cried last night, but that's just the vomiting, she thinks. She gets dressed. She wants to wear Shaw's shirt home like girls in the movies do, but then Shaw would have nothing to wear when he wakes up.

She walks toward Janey's room. She's surprised to see that Janey is awake, lying in bed on the phone. Janey waves when she sees Sethie, who comes inside and sits on the edge of the bed. Janey covers the mouthpiece. "Doug's going to bring over coffee—you want anything?"

Sethie shakes her head. "I should go home."

Janey nods. Sethie turns away as Janey gives Doug her order, flirts, and says good-bye.

"Shaw still asleep?" Janey asks. Sethie nods. Janey stretches her arms over her head.

"I can't believe you're not asleep," Sethie says. "You were up just a few hours ago." So very few hours ago, Sethie thinks, that the smell of cigarette smoke still hangs in Janey's room, despite their best efforts to blow it out the window.

Janey smiles. "So were you."

Sethie shrugs. She thinks Janey is smiling the same smile that she smiled at five in the morning, her smile for Doug.

"You really have to go?" Janey asks.

"English paper."

"Ugh," Janey moans, "I can't wait until this semester is over and our grades don't count anymore."

"Me too," Sethie says, though she can't imagine not trying to get As.

"Well, I'll wake Shaw up in a little while. You don't have to wait for him. No reason for his crap sleeping habits to affect your excellent work ones."

"Right," Sethie says. She wonders whether Shaw will be grumpy when Janey wakes him.

Janey walks Sethie to the elevator and gives her a hug. Sethie can smell the frat house in Janey's hair.

"I'll call you later," Janey promises as the elevator door slides shut.

When Sethie gets home, she can hear her mother in the shower behind the closed door of Rebecca's bedroom. Sethie heads to her own room, changes into pajamas, and comes out into the living room. She spreads her French homework on the coffee table and sits on the couch. The door to Rebecca's room is right off the living room, so when she finally opens it, she sees Sethie on the couch, conjugating verbs.

"Morning," Rebecca says.

"Hey."

It's past lunchtime, and Sethie lets her mother assume that she must have eaten at Janey's. Sethie's plan today is not to eat until dinner. She thinks it shouldn't be too difficult. On most weekdays, she gets up at seven and doesn't eat until eleven or twelve. So today, having gotten up in the middle of the day, it shouldn't be all that different to wait to have a single calorie until after six.

Her mother pulls some papers out from under Sethie's textbook on the coffee table; the FAFSA application, Sethie recognizes. She can't remember what FAFSA stands for, only that one of the As stands for "aid." Rebecca sits beside Sethie on the couch and begins paging through it, chewing on her bottom lip. When she is sure Rebecca won't see, Sethie looks at her mother. Rebecca sits with her legs folded underneath her, her feet bare. Sethie stares, for a few seconds, at Rebecca's feet. Rebecca has impossibly small feet. Sethie curls up the toes of her own—size eight and a half— and wonders why she didn't get feet like her mother's. A woman with size eight and a half feet will never be called dainty, or delicate, or even small.

Sethie notices Rebecca is only glancing over the financial aid forms. "You're going to fill that out, Mom, right?"

"Of course," Rebecca says. Sethie thinks she doesn't sound serious enough.

"You know the deadline?"

"Yes."

"I can write it down for you."

"Sethie," Rebecca says, sounding exasperated, "I know the deadline."

"Okay, but you know that you don't have to wait for the deadline. You can begin filling it out now." Sethie finished her college applications early, just as she finishes everything early. Rebecca is always late: late with the rent, with the tuition check to White, even though with Sethie's scholarship all Rebecca has to pay for is books and some incidentals, like the fees for class trips and yearbooks. Sometimes Sethie thinks Rebecca would forget altogether if she didn't remind her.

Rebecca says, "Don't worry about it."

"It's important," Sethie says. "And you shouldn't just leave it out on the coffee table, you know. You should put it somewhere safe."

"You could always get another one, if we needed it."

"It would be better if you kept it someplace safe," Sethie says. Sethie bought a special file folder for her application materials. Each college she's applying to has its own slot.

"Don't worry about it," Rebecca repeats.

Sethie shifts closer to the edge of the couch, even though there's still plenty of room between her and Rebecca. Sethie and her mother used to eat dinner on this couch, with the TV on, balancing their plates on their knees. They never really bothered with the dining room table. It never felt this crowded then, but that was before last winter, when Sethie went to the doctor for her annual checkup. Sethie thinks wryly that now she goes to the gynecologist, when less than a year ago her mother was still bringing her to a pediatrician. Even he said she was too old to keep going to him.

Sethie felt overly large in the exam room. Intended for younger patients, the table was so low to the ground that she couldn't even swing her legs when the doctor tried to check her reflexes. The ruler on the wall said she was 5'4"; the doctor said she was probably done growing, but not to rule out another inch in the next year or so. Sethie hoped not; she was already two inches taller than her mother, and when the doctor said her height out loud, Rebecca said that she could barely believe such a tall girl was her daughter. She'd said something similar the last time Sethie bought a bra; her breasts are larger than her mother's, too.

The scale in the corner sat there waiting. Sethie thought that weight was usually one of the first things they checked, but it seemed like even the doctor knew it was going to be a bad number; even he was putting it off: 132 pounds. Sethie must have looked crestfallen, because the doctor said, "Not the number you wanted to see, huh?" He didn't even reassure her that it was a perfectly healthy weight for her height, didn't allow for the fact that junior year can be very stressful, and who wouldn't want to grab a snack after school before practicing SAT words? No; it was not the number she wanted to see. At her last annual, it had been 115.

A girl isn't supposed to gain the freshman fifteen until she's actually a college freshman, Sethie thought. And a girl like me isn't supposed to gain it at all.

Her mother was in the room, of course. That's the policy at pediatricians' offices. That night, Sethie began to notice the way that her mother watched her, eyeing the way a certain tank top creased around her stomach, the way her legs looked sticking out from the bottom of a pair of the boxer shorts she slept in, as though Rebecca had been surprised at the number on the scale and was looking closely to see exactly how that had happened.

But then, Sethie thought, maybe she had always been

watching. Sethie imagined Rebecca's eyes, all that time, watching her eat pizza for dinner after she'd come home from SAT tutoring at the coffee shop, where she'd had hot chocolate with whipped cream. Because of Rebecca's long hours at work, she never cooked dinner; they always ordered in. Rebecca wouldn't have had hot chocolate, and she would order her pizza without pepperoni. Surely, Rebecca's hawk eyes had noticed every single pound she had gained after every yearbook meeting and every tutoring session.

Rebecca watched almost all the same shows that Sethie did, and after dinner, they would leave their dirty plates in the sink and watch TV on Rebecca's bed with the lights out. Sethie would lie on her side; at her heaviest, she felt how shallow the crook of her waist had become. During commercial breaks, she would press on it with her thumb. As she lost weight, she felt the crook deepen. She could fit the heel of her hand in it, and then her palm. But by then, she hated watching TV in Rebecca's room. By then, she could see that Rebecca thought, as she did, that she was still at fault for having gained the weight in the first place.

For her birthday this past summer, Sethie asked for a TV in her room.

Sethie bought a scale at the pharmacy around the corner a few weeks after seeing that 132. She'd already begun forcing back down the numbers that had crept so far up. Now, Sethie keeps the scale under her bed like contraband; Rebecca never knew she bought it. She steps on it every day, first thing in the morning, before taking her shower. She hasn't wanted to get on it today; she's sure that after last night, even with the vomiting, the number will be too high.

Rebecca doesn't need to keep a scale in the house. Rebecca is the type of woman who has never had to worry about gaining weight. Naturally thin, she would never understand how hard it is for Sethie to stop eating something delicious even when she's full. Sethie's mother is beautiful; beautiful, that is, for her age, which is 49. Beautiful in that way that 49-year-old women are beautiful, so that you know that once they were undeniably desirable girls. Sethie's mother's body has softened since she was younger; surely she's put on weight since her twenties and thirties. But still, there doesn't seem to be any fat on her. Sethie has seen pictures of Rebecca when she was in high school, her stomach taut in a two-piece. Sethie tries to imagine what it would be like to allow someone to take a picture of her with a bikini on. She tries to imagine wearing a bikini when there was anyone holding a camera in her sight line.

Now, Sethie closes her books and piles them together, picks them up.

"All done?" Rebecca asks, barely looking up from her papers.

"Yup," Sethie says, standing. She's lying; she's decided to finish her work in her room. Rebecca stretches her legs out in front of her, pointing and then flexing her toes. Her feet look, Sethie thinks, as perfect as a doll's.

# 9.

**BOYS LIKE SHAW** never say "I love you," but Sethie doesn't know if that means that Shaw loves her but doesn't like to talk about it, or if it means that he doesn't love her, because he's not the type to fall in love. She wonders what he would say if she told him she loved him. She wonders whether she does, in fact, love him. Since even the word *boyfriend* seems off-limits, she can only imagine how off-limits the word *love* is.

They're in her bedroom. Her mother is out for the evening, one of those law firm dinners. So Sethie's bedroom door is defiantly open.

Shaw is on the bed watching TV, and Sethie is sitting on the floor, leaning on the bed, drinking her liter of water. She's almost finished it, and she has to pee so badly she thinks she might burst. One more gulp, she promises herself, and you'll be done, and then you can go.

"Hey, gimme some of that," Shaw says, and before Sethie even realizes what he's doing, Shaw's taken the bottle out of her hand and drunk the last of the water. Sethie freezes; does this mean she can get up to pee? Should she get more water, try to approximate the amount Shaw drank, try to finish her task? She feels like she's trying to get away with something, like Shaw's just finished her homework for her, and she can't quite go through with handing in his work to the teacher.

But now Shaw rolls over to the edge of the bed, letting his arms hang down over her sides. His fingers trace shapes on Sethie's upper arms, and Sethie leans her head back. She tries to picture the shapes he's making; maybe he's writing words.

Then Shaw's fingers suddenly grab her, and he's pulling her up onto the bed with him. As he leans down over her, Sethie thinks the words, "Hold on one second" and "Let me just get up for a minute," but she can't make them come out of her mouth. What if she stops him, and when she comes back, he doesn't want her anymore? Sometimes Sethie thinks that the part of sex she most enjoys is that it proves Shaw wants her; she is scared that stopping him now will stop him wanting her later. So she lies there beneath him, even though her bladder feels like it's going to burst. When he's inside her, she thinks she can actually feel the liquid sloshing around. It hurts, and Sethie bites her lip to keep from crying. It's not Shaw's fault that it hurts; if he knew, he would stop. The first few times they slept together, he was so scared of hurting her. They had sex carefully, like each one thought they might break the other. It took them a while to realize the things they could do, the little pains that don't matter later. But even now, Shaw is gentle; he holds her face between his hands, he lifts her up carefully, he begins slowly. When they finish, he pulls the covers over her, because he knows she's always cold. Once, he joked that she must be the only girl whom sex made colder, not warmer. He doesn't know that's just from having his cold skin all over her. Sethie waits until Shaw is dozing, and then scrambles off the bed and into the bathroom.

Shaw doesn't leave until after ten. Once he's gone, Sethie washes her face and brushes her teeth. She carefully applies skin creams intended for much older women: anti-wrinkle cream for her eyes and her forehead, a special lip treatment to keep her lips plump and soft.

She changes into boxer shorts and a tank top and climbs into bed. She thinks she should sleep with long sleeves and long pants. Maybe that would prevent her current acrobat-ics. She has to fold the sheets between her legs, so that she won't feel the fat on her inner thighs rubbing together. She has to wrap her arms around a pillow, so that she won't feel the fat on her upper arms pressing into her sides. And she has to rest her cheek on that pillow the way she might rest it on Shaw's chest, if he were still here. She kisses the pillow where Shaw's cheek would be. Only then can she fall asleep.

**S**ETHIE HAS BEGUN helping Jancy with her English homework. Janey is determined to bring up her GPA this
semester.

"You get straight As," Sethie protests at first.

"Not in English," Janey insists. She has to bring out old
report cards before Sethie believes her.

Sethie teases Janey that her new interest in GPAs has to
do with getting into Columbia, to be close to Doug.

"Shut up," Janey says, laughing, but Sethie notices she
looks embarrassed and promises not to bring it up again,
and when she promises, Janey looks grateful.

"English lit is not my strong suit," Janey complains, but
Sethie spends at least one evening a week convincing Janey
that it could be her strong suit if she wanted it to be. After
a few weeks, Janey comes home with an A on a paper. She
shows it to Sethie the way that most kids would show it to
their parents.

"How did you do that?" Janey laughs, shoving the paper with the bright red A in Sethie's face.

"I didn't write the paper," Sethie says. "You did."

"Yeah, but I couldn't have done it without you. You're the kind of girl who always gets As."

"Not always. My B in art class pulled my whole GPA down last year."

Janey shakes her head and puts her arm around Sethie. "You make me feel like I can actually get As in English class."

"Well, obviously you can," Sethie says, laughing.

"Yeah, but I never thought so before."

❦ ❦ ❦

In November, Janey says Sethie should come over for Thanksgiving.

"I mean, you've already had a sampling of the Thanksgiving food at my house," she says, "so you know it's good."

Sethie is poring over a Chinese food menu in Janey's living room. Janey's parents are away again, or maybe still away is more accurate, though Janey says they came home for two days last week. Which has more calories, Sethie thinks, wonton soup or a spring roll?

"Oh, a spring roll, definitely." Sethie looks up; she hadn't realized she was thinking out loud. Janey continues, "And we'll order all the main courses with the sauce on the side. And brown rice, not white. Better for you."

Sethie nods, watching Janey stretch her arms over her

head as she reaches for the phone next to the couch. A stripe of Janey's white belly is visible between the bottom of her tank top and the top of her shorts. Sethie is trying to decide whether Janey has the type of body that could be described with words like *svelte* and *lithe*. Sethie has written those words on the full-length mirror in her bedroom with dry-erase marker. They are her two new favorite words; words that sound almost foreign; words whose meaning is obvious just from the shape of them in her mouth. The mirror is on the back of her door, so she doesn't have to worry about her mother seeing it; Rebecca would never be in Sethie's room with the door closed behind her. Usually, she stands just in the doorway without even coming inside at all. Sethie had also written *Don't Eat* and *Bones Are Beautiful;* but she erased those in favor of *svelte* and *lithe* a couple of weeks ago.

As Janey twists her body to pick up the phone, Sethie is frustrated because she didn't know that you could ask for Chinese food with the sauce on the side, and she's never eaten brown rice. She didn't even know that a spring roll was worse for her than soup; though when she thinks about it, of course it is. It's fried dough, after all. But then, soup sounds like so much more food than a spring roll. Sethie closes the menu angrily, like the Chinese-food people were trying to trick her.

"How did you know that, anyway—wonton soup versus spring roll?" Sethie asks, sighing. "You don't even count calories."

Janey shrugs. "Every girl goes through that phase,

doesn't she?" She says it like it's no big deal, like she's been there and now it's just Sethie's turn. Sethie does not like that Janey has just boiled the central preoccupation of her life down to a phase. A girl like Janey, Sethie thinks, has the luxury of it just being a phase; a girl like Janey is naturally thin, a girl like Janey can eat whatever she wants and never get fat. But Sethie knows that if she ever stops keeping track of what she eats, she will be fat. Not like Janey, born to be thin; Janey won the genetic lottery, and Sethie lost. This thought makes Sethie so angry that she is even hungrier.

Sethie concentrates on the way Janey knows the Chinese restaurant's number by heart, the way Janey orders expertly, and even seems to flirt with the guy on the other end of the line. When their food comes, there's a free order of spare ribs in there, a present for Janey's flirting. Sethie wishes Janey hadn't flirted; the spare ribs mean there is another food to contend with.

Before Sethie leaves, Janey says, "Don't forget about Thanksgiving. You can meet my parents." Janey laughs, like the concept of a friend meeting her parents is a joke. "And Doug will be there, so we won't be the only kids."

"Doug will be there?" Sethie asks.

"Yeah. His family lives in Virginia, and that's a little far for him to go just for the weekend. So he's coming here."

"His parents must miss him, though."

"Yeah, well, I think they were happy to hear he had a girlfriend." The word *girlfriend* comes out of Janey's mouth like a laugh. Sethie thinks, That was fast.

"Anyway," Janey says, "I'd like to have my real family with me for a change."

Sethie smiles, but she's thinking of the food that they'll have at Janey's Thanksgiving. She thinks about the stuffing and the gravy and the pie. She and her mother normally go to her mother's friend's house, since they don't do it at home, and there's not always traditional Thanksgiving food. There's only stuffing half the time and there's never pie. Thanksgiving at Janey's would definitely be more fattening, if more fun.

Sethie tries to imagine Shaw spending the holiday with them, like Doug is with Janey's family. Sethie can't picture him: passing the potatoes, sitting next to her, in a button-down and khakis or maybe just nice jeans, being polite to the grown-ups. Shaw would insist they sneak out early; he'd want to get stoned first so they could really enjoy the food.

But maybe Shaw will invite her to his place; his family is the type who does a big spread—very "the more the merrier." So Sethie doesn't ask her mother if she can go to Janey's, not for days. She's giving Shaw time to invite her to his place first, because if she's going to ask her mother to spend Thanksgiving with someone else, she'd like it to be Shaw. But then, it's the weekend before Thanksgiving, and Shaw hasn't asked, and Janey is still prompting her for an answer. Sethie lies and says she's already asked her mom. She says that her mother needs time to think about it; that her mother's being a pain in the ass, not letting her do her own thing.

The truth is, Sethie would be surprised if her mother didn't let her go. It's not like Thanksgiving is a big deal in their family. They don't dress up, and they take a cab to Rebecca's friend's house downtown. So when Sethie finally does ask, she's surprised at her mother's answer.

"Absolutely not."

Rebecca is sitting on the couch watching *Jeopardy!* Sethie waited until it went to commercial to ask.

"What?"

"No. Marcia's already ordered the food."

It takes Sethie a moment to understand her mother's logic. Marcia has already ordered the food she'll be serving on Thursday. It would be rude not to go when Marcia's already ordered Sethie her allotted amount. Sethie practically laughs. If only Marcia knew the trouble Sethie would go to to avoid eating her carefully ordered portion.

Sethie's mother would never think about limiting her portion. Sometimes Sethie wonders what her body would have ended up like if she'd never started messing with it; maybe she'd have ended up like Rebecca.

Even now, Sethie thinks, Rebecca would look better in a bathing suit than I would.

"I don't think food for one person really makes that big of a difference," Sethie says. She recalls that once, when it was snowing, they blew off Thanksgiving altogether. Sethie must have been eleven. Neither of them wanted to go out in the snow; Sethie's mother certainly didn't care about the food Marcia'd ordered then. They ordered in Chinese food and ate it on the couch, sharing a blanket. Sethie remembers that her mother was terrible with the chopsticks and dropped food on the couch. She'd laughed. "Isn't the kid supposed to be the sloppy one?" she'd said.

"It makes a difference to Marcia," Rebecca says, and Sethie thinks even her mother knows how lame her reasons sound, especially when she adds, "If it means that much to you, why don't you invite Janey to join us at Marcia's," which totally contradicts her point about the food Marcia's ordered.

Sethie can't figure out why her mother is so insistent that she spend this day with her, but she finally shrugs and goes back into her own room. She doesn't want to have to tell Janey; what a lame, childish thing it is to be kept from your friends by your mother. Janey's mother would never do that.

**11.**

**S**ETHIE IS LYING on the floor of her bedroom in her underwear, trying to figure out whether she is pretty. She holds a magnified mirror—the kind her mother keeps in the bathroom to put on her makeup—above her face and bends and straightens and shifts her arms so that she can see her face from every angle, every distance. Her pores are huge, but then, her lips look thick; her teeth are crooked, but her eyelashes are long. When she holds the mirror this close, she can just barely see her dark hair outlining her face, and her eyes look pale gray. She isn't sure whether her eyes are pretty, but she does conclude finally that they're striking, maybe even the kind of eyes that people talk about when you leave the room.

Sethie's room is a square. Her bed is in the corner, under the window; on the floor, Sethie lies parallel to it. She wouldn't even have to straighten her arms above her head to reach the nightstand above her while also touching the dresser on the other side of the room with her feet.

She resents any interruptions; the phone should not ring, homework does not need to be done. She is very busy lying on her back, enjoying the pain of her shoulders on the floor (that means she's bony), holding a mirror above her face. There are circles underneath her eyes. Are those ugly or mysterious? Heroin chic is out, so she decides they count as ugly. She presses down on the bump in her nose, a souvenir from a childhood accident. That makes her profile interesting, so she counts that as pretty. I should make a list, she thinks: pretty on one side, ugly on the other. Add it all up, and the column with more items wins. But then, some items should be worth more than just one point, she thinks. Like fat should be worth at least ten. Twenty, maybe. Maybe if there were some sort of scale that assigned value to each of the items, so that pretty could be objective like a math problem.

She hears her mother's footsteps on the hardwood floor outside her bedroom; it sounds like they're approaching her door. When the footsteps stop, Sethie listens, and she imagines her mother is listening too. Sethie stands up and walks back and forth between her bed and her desk a few times; she makes her footfalls heavy so that her mom will hear her and know she is perfectly all right inside the room, that there is no reason to knock on the door or come inside.

She waits until she can hear her mother's steps retreating; my mother, she thinks, has oddly audible footfalls for someone with such small feet. Sethie decides that she will learn to step lightly; no one will hear her enter a room. She will be so soft people will wonder what kind of magic allows her to keep a constant buffer of air between her feet and the ground. Her footfalls will be so light that it will make people think she is thinner than she is.

When Sethie can't hear the steps anymore, she lies back on the floor, straightens her arms, and tilts the mirror so that she can see only her collarbone, which doesn't protrude like it should, and then her breasts, spilling out the sides of her bra. She tilts the mirror again so that she can see her stomach and the tops of her hips; all the soft places that should be smooth, and tight, and hard. I don't have a pretty enough face, Sethie thinks, to make up for the fat on my body; but I don't have a good enough body to make up for the flaws in my face.

A few months before Sethie turned thirteen, her mother arranged her bat mitzvah. Evil tradition, Sethie thinks now, paraded around in front of friends and family right when you're most awkward; a year of invitations and snubs around school during the time when everyone's most insecure about who likes whom and who doesn't. The way she remembers it, she invited the girls she wished were her friends as much as she did any of the girls who actually were.

And an evil tradition, because it's right when you're likely in the middle of a growth spurt, and a dress bought and fitted months ahead of time is likely not to fit on the big day. She remembers the way her dress rubbed under her armpits; she felt as though she'd grown before she ought to have. Because of her recent growth, the dress was also shorter than it was meant to be. She was wearing her first pair of high heels, and panty hose with a sheen, just like her mother wore. One of the girls came up to her during the party and said, "It's okay that your dress is so short, Sethie—you've got great legs!" It was a compliment, of course, but that night, Sethie went home and appraised herself in the mirror for the first time, especially her legs. They had looked better with the hose and the high heels than they did bare. If pressed, she'd have to admit that her bat mitzvah was the day when her body became what it is now: an endless source of fascination and disappointment.

Sethie presses the heel of her hand against the side of her stomach. There, right there; that soft piece just shouldn't be there. She pinches it for emphasis. A useless piece of flesh, she thinks disgustedly, pulling it away from her body. I ought to be able to just cut if off. She drops the mirror now, and presses both sides of her torso, then pinches the fat. Yes, she thinks, I should just cut the fat right out.

She sits up and pinches her inner thighs. It's so clear where the muscle ends and the fat begins. It'd be like liposuction. It's not like she needs that fat. There's a scab above her right knee, where she cut herself shaving. I could start there, she thinks. Make that hole bigger and then just reach in, and scrape out the fat with my nails.

She puts the mirror down, and places her hands on either side of the scab. It's so easy she barely has to move; the scab flicks right off. And then she scratches the place where the scab used to be, bending her leg to get closer.

She leans closer, feeling where her stomach rolls when she bends over. She sits back up and sucks her stomach in, then leans down again.

Blood tastes like metal. She wanted to discover something more romantic than that; that it tasted sweet or rich, that it oozed out from her skin like the melted part in the middle of a molten chocolate cake. But Sethie's blood does not ooze; it isn't slow and rich. It is thin, running down her leg, as if it can't wait to get away from her.

Sethie's blood is disappointing. She spits it into the garbage can by her desk. She's glad she didn't swallow it: for all she knows, blood might have calories.

She sits up and leans back against the bed, cups her hand beneath her thigh to catch her blood. It's almost stopped bleeding anyway.

She jumps when the phone rings. The blood on her hand has dried, though, so it doesn't spill onto the floor. The metal taste is fresh in her mouth, but this time it's adrenaline, not blood. She doesn't realize that every time her phone rings, she holds her breath before she picks it up, because every time the phone rings, it might be Shaw.

**J**ANEY SAYS EVERYONE is going back up to Columbia tonight and Sethie has to come. "Get dressed. Everyone's waiting for us."

Sethie feels guilty that she's made everyone wait while she was inspecting herself in the mirror, even though until this very moment she didn't know she was going up to Columbia tonight. She's not entirely sure who "everyone" is, but she thinks it means Shaw will be there.

"What are you wearing?" Sethie asks.

"Jeans and a funky top. I'm hanging up now, and I'm going to get into a cab—meet me on your corner in five minutes."

"Five minutes isn't enough time to get ready, Janey! It's barely enough time to get downstairs." Sethie feels genuinely panicked. She still has to wash the dried blood off her leg and hand.

"Sure it is, when a girl's as gorgeous as you are. See you in five."

For a second, Sethie stares at the phone in her hand. She doesn't understand why she has to go up there with Janey anyway. Shaw's never been on time since she's known him; she bets that if she could only wait for Shaw, she'd have all the time in the world. But Janey will be in her elevator by now, and on her way.

Sethie scoots across the floor and opens her jeans drawer. No one will be able to see the blood with her jeans on anyhow.

⚜ ⚜ ⚜

"Not bad for five minutes, young lady," Janey says. Sethie wishes she'd had more time to get ready. Clearly, Janey spent plenty of time applying the black liner around her eyes, and Sethie's own makeup feels messy and inadequate by comparison. Sethie tried doing her makeup like Janey's yesterday before school, but it didn't look the same on her. The black eyeliner made her eyes seem too round, almost somehow far away from the rest of her face. And her hair kept getting caught in the Vaseline she smeared on her lips; Sethie remembered later that Janey keeps her hair mostly pulled back. The makeup was odd on Sethie, as though people would be able to tell, even without ever having seen her before, that this wasn't what she usually looked like. So tonight she rubbed pink gloss on her lips and chocolate brown mascara on her lashes. She pressed blush onto her cheeks and powder onto her eyelids. She'd wanted to add brown eyeliner, but there wasn't enough time.

Janey's moved on to other things.

"They have parties almost every weekend. The school hates it, but their house is technically off campus, so there's nothing they can do."

Sethie nods. She thought all frat houses had parties.

"Doug says it's the best house on campus."

"I thought you said it was off campus." Sethie blinks.

"Well, technically, sure, but I just mean—the best house of any of the fraternities up there."

Sethie nods. She guesses that's important. Even though it's freezing, she rolls the taxi window all the way down. She hasn't eaten much today, and the cool air wakes her up a little. She should get some coffee, she thinks. Or a Diet Coke—no calories. It'll be a late night.

§ § §

Janey walks into the frat house like she's a regular, which Sethie guesses she is now. Janey and Doug have been together for nearly two months. Janey pulls Sethie toward the stairs—she wants to go straight up to Doug's room. Sethie wants to look around to see whether Shaw has gotten here yet, so she lags behind. She sees him over on a couch by the window. She smiles.

"Wait," she says to Janey. "I want to say hi to Shaw." She drops Janey's hand.

Shaw doesn't realize she's there until she's right next to him. "Hey," she says. She wants to lean down to kiss him hello, but she doesn't think he'd like that. So she waits.

Shaw raises his eyebrows. "Hey!" he says loudly. "When did you get here?"

"Just now, with Janey."

"Oh," Shaw says, nodding. Shaw swings his arm from the back of the couch where it had been resting; for a second she thinks he might take her hand, pull her down onto his lap. Instead, he gestures to the girl and the guy sitting next to him. "This is Anna, and you know Jeff Cooper, right?" Sethie nods. She guesses Jeff and Anna are a couple, but it's hard to tell; the couch is so small that they're all three sitting very close.

"Tell Janey not to go getting into too much trouble up there," Shaw says, stretching his arm back behind the couch and nodding toward the stairwell. Sethie thinks she's supposed to leave now; Shaw has sent her away with a message.

"Okay," she says, "I will." She thinks Shaw looks pissed, but she's not sure why.

§ § §

Sethie can't remember exactly which room is Doug's, and now Janey's gone, so there's no one to show her the way. She's scared of walking into the wrong room, but she knows she looks like an idiot hovering outside three closed doors. She strains her ears until she thinks she hears Janey's laugh. She follows the sound and feels very brave when she turns the doorknob and very lucky when she gets it right.

"Sethie!" Janey squeals as she opens the door. She jumps up from her spot on the couch. "You found us!"

Janey kisses her on the cheek, her lips sticky and hot. "Everybody, this is my best friend Sethie. Isn't she pretty?"

Sethie isn't sure why Janey is addressing "everybody"— the only people in the room are Doug and one other boy. Janey gives her labels quickly, if not lightly: Sethie is already her best friend, Doug already her boyfriend. But it feels good to be called someone's best friend. Sethie hasn't been called that since elementary school, when she had a new best friend every month or so.

Janey takes her hand. "Sit here," she says, leading Sethie toward a small couch that Sethie thinks is technically a love seat, though she can't imagine anyone here would call it that. "You'll make room for her, right?" Janey says to the lanky boy propped in the corner, who nods. Sethie sits.

Janey takes her seat across from Sethie, next to Doug on the bed, whose arm goes around her almost automatically. Sethie bets they kissed hello too.

"Is Sethie short for something?"

"What?" Sethie says, turning her head from Doug and Janey.

The lanky boy on the couch next to her repeats his question. "Is Sethie short for something?"

Sethie nods. "Yup. What's your name?"

Lanky Boy smiles. "You didn't tell me what Sethie was short for."

Sethie smiles back. "You didn't ask."

Lanky Boy smiles wider. "You're pretty clever, aren't you?"

"Yes, actually, as a matter of fact, I am." Sethie can't quite believe she just said that. It's the kind of snappy comeback Janey would come up with, not her. She decides that Lanky Boy must be an excellent conversationalist.

"So what is your name?" she asks again.

"Ben."

Sethie nods.

"So what is Sethie short for?"

Sethie pauses before answering. She could try for another snappy comeback. But rather than press her luck, she says, "Sarah Beth."

Ben cocks his head to the side like he's considering that. "Is Beth your middle name or part of your first name?"

"Middle."

"So why not Sarah?"

Sethie purses her lips, feeling how dry they are. Her lip gloss has already worn off. Not like Janey's.

"Don't know."

"Hasn't anyone ever asked that before?"

Sethie smiles, and then laughs. "Nope, no one ever has."

"So I'm your first," Ben says, raising his eyebrows.

Still laughing, Sethie says, "Sure, you could call it that."

Sethie looks back at Doug and Janey, who are smiling and whispering, glancing over at them. She's sure they're talking about her, but she can't imagine about what, or why. For once, at least for now, she doesn't care. She feels warm, and the couch is soft, and Ben's long arms and legs make her feel small beside him. And small is almost skinny. Ben hands her a beer.

"Thanks." She takes it, but she doesn't open it.

"The way it works," Ben says, "is that you pop back that little tabby there—"

Sethie scowls at him. "I'm familiar with the mechanics of cans."

"Well then, let 'er rip."

"No. I haven't decided whether I'm going to drink it yet."

"Why's that?"

"I haven't eaten much today, so I'm going to have to pace myself." Sethie can't help but feel a nice little poke of pride when she says she hasn't eaten much today, just like that, like it's no big deal, she's just a regular skinny girl who can skip the occasional meal without thinking about it, longing for it, imagining what it might have been and how many calories it might have had.

"Well, we can't have that," Ben says, "slip of a thing like you." He reaches his arms across the couch, over Sethie. She leans back into the couch as much as she can. His fingers almost touch her breasts, but she holds her breath.

"Here," he says. He's grabbed a bag of chips from the table on Sethie's side of the couch. Sethie hadn't known they were there, but now that they're in front of her, her mouth is watering. How could they have been there that whole time, she wonders, without her having noticed?

"Ooh," Janey says, reaching for the bag. "Yum." She turns to Doug. "Can we get some pizza from that place?"

"Sure," Doug says, but Sethie's thinking, what place? Janey wouldn't say "that place" unless she'd had its pizza already. But Janey has been coming up here regularly, to see Doug, because she's his girlfriend.

"Sethie, you're going to love this pizza," Janey says. She stands up and walks to the window, perches on the sill, lights a cigarette. Sethie gets up to stand beside her. Chips and pizza, she thinks. And beer. Maybe a cigarette will help keep her from eating the chips at least until the pizza gets here.

But the cigarette burns down quickly, and then Janey is reaching her hand into the bag for some chips. Sethie watches her friend, watches her chin move as she chews, imagines the texture of the chip changing from hard to soft in her mouth. Digestion starts in the mouth, she thinks. The more you chew, the better. But Janey doesn't look like she's thinking about digestion, or calories, as she reaches into the bag again.

Sethie thinks Janey must be faking it. Even if she said that was just a phase she once went through. There can't be a girl left who doesn't at least fleetingly consider fat every time she eats. Only boys and little kids can do that.

Sethie decides she will fake it too. Just for now. Just for a few chips. Just until the pizza comes.

But then, what constitutes a few chips? Is that as many as you can fit before the pizza gets here? Because that's how many Sethie's eating. She barely puts one in her mouth before her other hand reaches back into the bag. She's scared that Janey or Doug or Ben will notice, will make a joke about the girl who can't stop eating. She can't help herself: she is so hungry. The salt of the chips is the first real taste she's had in her mouth all day; it tastes so strong, her eyes tear. She tries to force herself to wait in between chips; she can only take another chip after someone else has taken one. This rule slows her down a bit.

The pizza has pepperoni. Little pools of oil have formed on top of the cheese, in between the slices. Sethie thinks it's interesting that some foods even look like fat before they've made their way into your body and onto your inner thighs, your upper arms, the sides of your torso. And she thinks it's pathetic, really, how even with all that fat floating on the surface, she's still reaching for a piece of pizza.

I should hate myself more, Sethie thinks. If I hated myself enough, then I could stop eating altogether.

Two slices down. But she didn't eat the crusts, and she took some of the cheese off the second one. She wishes there were salt; maybe, if she salted the second slice too much, it wouldn't taste so good and she'd be able to put it down.

Doug's on his third slice; Ben too. Janey's still working on her first, because she'd stopped halfway through it to pour drinks. She pours a shot of something pink and sticky for Sethie. Sethie drinks it; she knows alcohol is fattening, but this drink burns on the way down like it's going to swim after all the food in her stomach and make it dissolve.

Sethie stands up and lights another cigarette. She smokes it too fast; for a second she feels nauseous, and the nausea makes her remember that she can undo everything she just did. Every last calorie could get up from inside of her. She wants to hurry, before anything begins to digest.

It shouldn't be hard, she thinks. Just ask where the bathroom is. You kind of have to pee anyway. She wills herself to feel nauseous.

"Where's the bathroom?" she asks, quietly, like it's no big deal, like the words don't take up all the space in her mouth, like the words themselves aren't the beginning of what she's about to do.

"I'll show you," Ben says, standing up. He hadn't stood up until now, and he's so tall that Sethie's head hits her back when she tilts her neck to look up at him. He's taller than Shaw, but not any wider. Just longer. He puts his hand on Sethie's back to lead her out the door, and she nearly leans against him, even though she's not so drunk that she can't stand up on her own. Someone this tall doesn't seem like he belongs out in the world.

"How tall are you?" she asks.

Ben smiles. "Six seven," he says. Sethie thinks he sounds almost embarrassed.

Sethie tries to calculate; if he's six seven, then Shaw can't be more than five ten, right? Not nearly as tall as she always thought he was. Not like Ben, who is something out of a fairy tale. The giant who should frighten you but who is actually gentle, and kind, and good. The character who actually saves the day.

Sethie keeps her head tilted up at Ben even as they walk down the hall. She doesn't even notice that he's opened the bathroom door for her, and is gesturing for her to go in.

"Sarah Beth," he says. "Here you are. Sorry it's such a mess."

"I guess you get sick of answering."

"Answering what?"

"When people ask how tall you are."

Ben shrugs. "I'm used to it."

"But you still get sick of it, don't you?"

Ben smiles and nods. Sethie says, "You should say you're five ten. Just to mess with people."

Ben laughs. "I'll try that."

Sethie smiles at him. "Your friends must all have sore necks," she says.

Ben grins back. "Yeah, well, I have sore shoulders from bending down so much, so it's fair."

Sethie nods. "You're right, it's fair."

Just for a second, Sethie wishes she were taller, so that she could be the friend who doesn't make Ben's shoulders ache. It's a strange wish, and it doesn't last long; all Sethie's ever wanted is to be smaller; one of her favorite things about Shaw is how small he makes her feel. When she steps inside the bathroom, she has to remind herself why she's there.

It's a real bathroom, not just a collection of stalls: there's a bathtub, a sink, and the toilet. She looks at the bathtub first. There are half a dozen shampoos lined up inside; three or four towels are hanging over the shower curtain rod. This shower must service all the guys who live on this floor, and she wonders if it gets crowded in the morning and how they decide who gets to use it first and what they do if someone uses up someone else's shampoo.

The sink is crowded with toothbrushes and toothpaste. They all look the same to her. She wonders if she'll get to college and accidentally use someone else's toothbrush. She decides no matter what, she'll keep her toiletries in her room. Though surely sorority houses and girls' dorms are in better shape than this.

She's avoiding the toilet. She's scared of how dirty it's going to be, scared to crouch down in front of it, resting her knees in the same spot where dozens of boys have missed the bowl. She looks around for a toilet brush. There's some Mr. Clean next to the tub, and she grabs it. She points it at the toilet, still standing a couple of feet away. She wishes this were at least antibacterial cleaner.

She decides she's being a baby. She's not actually going to touch the toilet, after all, and she'll keep her eyes closed. Really, only her knees are going to touch the ground, and they're protected by her jeans.

And so she crouches. She keeps her eyes closed. She puts her hand in her mouth, and her fingernails scratch against the top. She wiggles her fingers until she gags. Dammit, she thinks, I should have rolled up my sleeves.

Vomiting happens in waves. First, she sees red. The tomato sauce. It comes up easy, smooth. So does the pink alcohol. But then there are white chunks—the bottom of the pizza, pieces barely even chewed. She shakes her head at herself; she's supposed to be better about chewing. She thinks the chips will be next. If she can just get to the chips, she decides, she can stop. Only one more, she tells herself.

She raises her hand to her mouth and parts her lips.

She presses her fingers against her teeth; they won't un-clench. She almost laughs when she thinks that she might have to pry her own teeth apart.

Come on mouth, she thinks, just one more time. Then I promise, I'll stop. She closes her eyes. If she weren't in front of a toilet, it would look like she was praying. Or begging. Which she is—begging her mouth to open.

Someone knocks on the door.

"Just a second," Sethie calls out. Her mouth opened easily then, but her voice sounds hoarse.

"Sethie, it's me, let me in," Janey's voice calls out.

Shit, Sethie thinks, standing up. Her hand is covered in vomit, and when she flushes the toilet some of it falls onto the seat, some of it sticks on the flush lever. There are no paper towels in here, so she reaches for the toilet paper, and when she wipes up the mess, pieces of it stick to her hand.

"Sethie, let me in! I have to pee."

Sethie looks around her. She doesn't think Janey will be able to tell what she's been doing in here. As she steps to-ward the door, she sees her face. Her eyes are bright red; it looks like she's been crying. Her cheeks are wet, and she doesn't know whether it's from tears or backsplash from the toilet. There's a piece of vomit in her hair; she brushes it out with her fingers.

She doesn't know why she's so bothered by the idea of Janey's finding out what she's been doing. Janey was the one who taught her to do it, after all.

"Just a second," Sethie says again, but quietly, so that

Janey can't possibly hear. She opens the door, and Janey steps in. She's moving quickly, drunk and excited. Sethie walks to the sink to wash her hands while Janey pees.

"I just love it here, Sethie, don't you? There are always people around, even when you're just upstairs in Doug's room and not down at the party."

Sethie nods. She leans over the sink, cupping water in her hands and trying to drink it before it slips between her fingers. The water isn't cold, and the warmth feels good on her throat.

"You were gone so long the boys were joking about it. But I explained that skinny girls sometimes need time in the bathroom after a junk food binge like that."

Sethie's head snaps up. She looks at Janey, who's crouched above the toilet, trying not to let her thighs touch the seat. Sethie can't believe she told them—like it was nothing, no big deal, just something that all skinny girls do.

"How's your stomach feel?" Janey asks, pulling up her pants.

"Huh?"

"Your stomach? I swear to God, when I eat like that, sometimes I wonder why I ever eat anything, my stomach hurts so much."

Sethie doesn't say anything. Janey thought she had a stomachache.

Janey stands close to Sethie now, washing her hands, sharing the sink. She turns and looks closely at Sethie's eyes. Sethie doesn't say anything. Maybe Janey will think that her stomach hurt so much she was crying.

"Oh," Janey says finally. "I can't believe you did that here."

"Why not?"

Janey looks around her, wrinkling her nose. Janey would never get down on this floor. Janey would never crouch over that toilet. Well, fuck Janey, Sethie thinks, Janey doesn't have to.

"You don't understand," Sethie says.

Janey shrugs. "I guess I can't really blame you for it."

Janey must mean that given how much she saw Sethie eat, she can hardly blame her for needing to throw it up. Even Janey is disgusted by the way she shoveled all that food in.

Janey adds, "I showed you how, after all."

Sethie nods.

"Just, you know, be careful. Try not to make a habit out of it."

Sethie nods.

"Come here," Janey says, directing Sethie to the tub and sitting her down on its edge. "Let's fix your makeup." Janey reaches into her purse. Sethie looks up at Janey's face obediently.

"Feels like you're my big sister," Sethie says before she can stop herself.

But Janey just says, "I know," and runs a Q-tip under Sethie's eyes.

"How do you just happen to have all that stuff in your purse?"

"Well, I need it for tomorrow," Janey says. "I'm going to stay over."

Sethie nods. Of course Janey's staying over.

"Don't worry, though. Ben will put you in a cab. I bet he'll even ride home with you, just to make sure you get there safely. He's a really nice guy."

Sethie shakes her head. "I'll leave with Shaw." With Shaw, she repeats to herself. It feels like it's been a long time since she even thought his name, let alone said it out loud. But it can't have been more than just a couple hours since she saw him downstairs.

"Shaw left." Sethie looks down so fast that Janey pokes her in the eye with the Q-tip.

"Jesus, Sethie, be careful."

"Sorry," Sethie says, looking back up. Her eyes are wet, but Janey doesn't comment. Janey must think that it's from the Q-tip in her eye, or the vomiting, or both.

"Anyway, I don't need Ben to take me home."

"He won't mind," Janey says, smiling now. Sethie thinks she can see Janey's collarbone spark as she leans over her.

"Well, I don't mind going home alone," Sethie says.

"Sethie," Janey says, sounding exasperated. "Seriously. Ben wants to take you home."

"Why would he want to take me home?"

Janey wrinkles her nose. "I know I just found you with your head practically in the toilet, but Jesus, do you really think so little of yourself? He likes you."

Sethie leans back now, away from Janey's hands fixing her makeup. She almost loses her balance and falls into the tub.

"Well, if he likes me," she says deliberately, "all the more reason for him not to take me home. I don't want to lead him on."

"Why would you be leading him on?" Janey asks. She walks to the mirror now, brings her hands to her own face, fixes her own hair.

"We should get going anyway," Sethie says. "The boys will wonder what we're up to."

Janey shrugs. "Okay, Sethie. But don't you like Ben back?"

"I didn't think of him like that," Sethie says.

"You didn't? You were flirting with him. I thought you liked him. Doug was patting himself on the back over it."

"What do you mean, Doug was patting himself on the back. Was he—were you trying to set me up? Why would you do that?"

"I thought it'd be fun if we were both dating guys here. Think of all the time we could spend together!"

"Well, that's not a bad plan," Sethie says, trying to sound lighthearted. "But I'm not going to break up with Shaw just so that we can share cabs across town."

Janey cocks her head. "Break up with Shaw?" she repeats.

"Janey, you know that Shaw and I are . . ."

"Screwing?"

"Shit, Janey, you know that Shaw's my . . ."

"Fuck buddy?"

"Jesus Christ, Janey, why are you making me spell it out? Shaw's my boyfriend, and you know it."

Maybe it's the acoustics of the bathroom, but the word *boyfriend* sounds hollow, tinny in Sethie's ears. It sounds like it doesn't mean anything at all. It certainly doesn't sound like she thought it would when she finally said it for the first time.

Janey looks like she feels sorry for Sethie, but Janey doesn't know what Shaw's like when they're alone. Janey doesn't know that Shaw puts extra blankets on the bed when Sethie comes over so that she won't get too cold.

"Ben is a really good guy," Janey says finally. "I thought you should know what that was like."

Like I'm the pity case that you set up with the "nice guy," Sethie thinks but doesn't say. Instead she says, "I'm sure he is, but I'm already dating a nice guy," and opens the bathroom door.

She hears Janey mutter, "No, you're not," and she doesn't know whether Janey means that Shaw isn't a nice guy or that Sethie isn't dating him.

Sethie wishes she could leave right now, but her coat and her purse are in Doug's room. She turns away from the stairs and toward his door. Janey follows close behind. "I'm going home," Sethie says.

"Okay," Janey says as they walk into Doug's room. "I'll walk you to the corner to catch a cab."

Sethie leans over Ben to grab her coat and purse off Doug's couch. She shakes her head.

"Sethie, I'm not letting you walk out by yourself. It's after midnight."

Sethie shakes her head again. "You'd have to walk back alone then, anyway."

She thinks Ben and Doug are exchanging looks, trying to figure out if this is some kind of girl code so that Ben will volunteer to walk her out. Too late, Sethie realizes she should have let Janey walk her.

"I'll walk you out," Ben says, standing up. He leans down over Sethie. " 'Bout time I left these two lovebirds alone anyway." Sethie smiles back at him. After all, it's not Ben's fault. And Janey looks genuinely sorry as she gives her a hug good-bye.

Sethie can't help thinking that Doug looks like an idiot, quite pleased with himself because Ben is walking her out, just like he'd hoped, and he's going to be alone with Janey, just like he probably wanted all night.

Sethie has to admit, as Ben holds open the front door for her, that he doesn't seem like a pity-nice-guy kind of setup. He walks slightly in front of her, and he's so tall that he can block the wind; he's not wearing a coat, but the cold doesn't seem to bother him.

"Does everyone think you play basketball?"

"Yeah."

"Do you get sick of that question too?"

"Not as sick as I get of always being the one to change the lightbulbs."

Sethie laughs. "Oh my God, me too!"

Ben looks down at her as if to point out that she's still much too short to reach the ceiling.

"My mom, I mean. She's littler than I am. So I always get stuck with doing things around the house."

"Like being tall automatically makes you the handyman."

"I guess. When there's only girls in the house."

"Where's your dad?"

"California."

Ben nods like that makes perfect sense. He says, "I still have to stand on a chair."

"Me too. So it's really no easier for us than it would be for them. Pisses you off, doesn't it?" Sethie asks, cocking her head to look up at him.

"Sometimes, yeah."

"Yeah."

"Never thought I'd meet a girl who felt like that, though."

Sethie shrugs, and they lapse into silence.

"Aren't you cold?" she asks finally, to make conversation as he walks her to the corner of Broadway.

Ben shakes his head. "Nah. Grew up in Vermont. These NYC wimps don't even know real cold." Sethie giggles.

"See," he says. He stops walking and reaches for her hand. "Feel." He slips her fingers underneath his sleeve so that they brush against his forearm.

"Oh," Sethie can't help whispering. Ben's arm is perfectly warm. Her fingers curl around it.

"Damn, girl. You're freezing." He doesn't say it like the cold of her fingers bothers his warm skin; he says it as an offer to warm her up. "Here," he says, and he moves his arm so that it's wrapped around her, and his arms are so long that he's able to take her left hand in his left and her right in his right, and his hands are so large that they cover hers completely, like gloves.

This isn't holding hands, she thinks, because she isn't holding his at all. Her hands are balled up into fists under his.

When they get to a corner, Sethie realizes that Ben will have to let go of her in order to hail a cab. But even when he drops her right hand, she still feels like he's covering her completely.

"There you are, Sarah Beth," Ben says as a cab slows to a stop in front of them.

"Here I am," she says, and when he leans over to open the cab door, she finds that she's facing him, her back to the open door, looking up at him like girls do at the end of dates, when they're expecting to be kissed. Ben is standing close to her, but he doesn't kiss her; instead, he puts his hand on her shirt, over her stomach. Sethie inhales sharply; normally she hates being touched on her stomach. When Shaw puts his hand on her stomach, Sethie leans away from him, curls her shoulders over to make her stomach seem concave. But Ben's hand is so large that it makes her stomach feel small, and Sethie has to fight the urge to puff her stomach out, to lean forward, just to fill up his hand. Maybe then he could curl his fingers around it and pull her toward him.

But he's not pulling her toward him. He's actually

guiding her into the cab, pushing her away from him. She is almost surprised to find herself sitting in the taxi, and the door closed behind her. She doesn't remember saying good-bye, but they must have.

The cabdriver asks her where she's going, and she gives him her address. At a red light, he turns back to look at her and says, "That's your honey, huh?"

It takes her a second to realize what he's asking.

She shakes her head. "No."

The cabdriver laughs. "Maybe he will be."

Sethie shakes her head again. Ben is not her honey. Ben is the friendly giant; giants are never the heroes at the beginning of stories.

Her stomach still feels warm.

**S**ETHIE IS READING a memoir by a girl who was both anorexic and bulimic. She gets some good ideas from it, like drinking a full glass of water before each meal will make her feel full faster and eating very spicy foods can speed up her metabolism. Sethie looks at the picture of the author; it's a full-body picture, and takes up the entire back cover, as though the author wants readers to know that even though she's better now, even though she's stopped doing all those bad things she talks about in the book, she's still thin. Sethie can't ever stop; she knows the minute she stops, she will get fat.

Sethie waits until Tuesday, three days after she saw Shaw sitting on the couch with Jeff Cooper and that girl. On Tuesday, she waits for school to end, waits until the teachers let her go and the hands on the clock in the senior lounge roll around to the appropriate hour. She leaves school so fast she forgets her French textbook and will have to come in early the next day to finish her homework. She hasn't spoken to Shaw since she saw him at the fraternity house on Saturday night, since she left without him, since she almost imagined herself kissing Ben.

Shaw is on the corner outside his school, lighting a cigarette. Sethie can see him from across the street; he's looking down at Janey. Sethie stands still, even when the light changes and she's blocking the way for the people standing behind her. She can see that Janey looks angry and Shaw looks impatient.

It looks, Sethie can tell, like Janey is doing all the talking. Shaw is mostly shaking his head and shrugging. Sethie wonders what they're fighting about. She decides it would be better to cross the street and interrupt their fight than to have them look up and see her staring at them. So she begins walking, but slowly. Maybe if she takes her time they'll wrap this up before she gets there.

As she gets closer, she hears Janey say, "Look, Shaw, I'm trying to do the right thing here. But I'm not going to keep quiet about this forever," and Shaw shrugs and inhales on his cigarette and looks up to blow out the smoke and that's when he sees Sethie.

"Hey," Sethie says, lifting her hand to wave even though now she's standing next to them. She thinks how much younger she must look, wearing a school uniform next to their regular clothes.

"Hey," Shaw and Janey say in near perfect unison, and then Janey takes a step toward her and grabs her arm.

"Come on," she says, pulling Sethie to the corner.

Sethie looks back at Shaw, but she thinks that Janey's going to explain the fight to her, so she doesn't pull away.

But instead of talking to her, Janey's putting her into a cab and climbing in after her.

"113th and Broadway," Janey says.

"Wait," Sethie says, "I was supposed to see Shaw."

"Huh?" Janey asks, distracted. "What for?"

"What do you mean what for? Janey, you don't get to decide which friends I hang out with."

Janey considers this and then says, "You're right, I'm sorry. I'm just kind of mad at Shaw right now."

"Well, that's between you and Shaw, not you and me, right?"

Janey doesn't say anything. She rolls down the window and leans on the glass, so the top of her head sticks out of the car. Sethie thinks her friend looks guilty, but she can't imagine about what.

"What were you guys fighting about?" Sethie asks finally.

Janey shrugs. "I don't remember anymore."

"I don't believe you," Sethie says, and for the briefest moment, an image of Shaw and Janey together flashes in Sethie's head. Janey is so comfortable around him: grabbing his belt, sharing his drinks.

"Is something going on between you and Shaw?" Sethie says quickly, before she can decide not to ask. "Is that why you were trying to set me up with Ben? You were feeling guilty?"

"What?" Janey says, rolling up the window. "Jesus Christ, Sethie, what's gotten into you?"

Sethie shrugs, and the cab stops on 113th Street, at the very same spot where she said good-bye to Ben a few days earlier.

"Come on," Janey says, opening the door. Sethie slides out after her. As she follows Janey toward the frat house, she thinks that they better be leaving here before dinnertime, because she allowed herself a whole bagel for lunch based on a plan to have sushi for dinner, and she's pretty sure that if they have dinner up here it won't be anything healthy like sushi.

On the steps of the frat house, Janey rings the doorbell, and while they wait for Doug to let them in, Janey says, "You're right, though."

"I'm right?"

"I am feeling guilty."

Sethie looks at the ground. She doesn't want to see what her best friend's face looks like when she tells her that she's sleeping with her boyfriend.

"It's not what you think, though."

"No?" Sethie murmurs, studying her shoes.

"I didn't realize just how seriously you were taking things with Shaw."

Sethie doesn't say anything. Janey made it perfectly clear the other night that she didn't think Shaw and Sethie were serious. And maybe then, maybe then it doesn't count; maybe then, if they're sleeping together, it's not a betrayal, because maybe Janey really did think that Shaw didn't belong to Sethie. And maybe Shaw thought that they didn't belong to each other. Maybe Sethie's the one who's really got it all wrong here. So maybe she has no right to be mad at all right now. Maybe she had no reason to feel guilty for almost imagining kissing Ben.

"Hey, guys," Doug says, opening the door. He looks surprised to see Sethie, and Janey looks like she's trying not to cry.

Sethie surprises herself by saying, "I came to see Ben. Is he around?"

"Yeah," Doug says. "He'll be psyched to see you. His room's on the third floor, right below where mine is."

"Okay then," Sethie says, and steps into the house. She wants to have more time before Janey tells all. For a little bit longer, she wants to be a girl who has a best friend and a boyfriend. She stops to go the bathroom on her way to Ben's room, just to look in the mirror, just to see herself that way again. She smiles into the mirror, like there's someone on the other side waiting to take her picture.

Sethie can't quite believe she's knocking on Ben's door.

"Come in," she hears him say. His voice is very deep, a little hoarse, like maybe he's coming down with a cold.

Ben doesn't look up when she opens the door. He's sitting on his bed, bent over a textbook. His legs are crossed, but you can still tell that he's far taller than the bed is; you can tell that he probably has to sleep curled up in a ball so that his legs don't hang over the edge, that he probably wakes up with knees sore from having been bent all night.

"You ever feel like Goldilocks?"

Ben looks up. He looks surprised to see Sethie in his doorway, but he doesn't miss a beat and replies, "Doesn't she complain that the beds are too soft and too hard, not too big or too small?"

"Close enough."

Ben shrugs. "Close enough," he repeats.

"Ever get tired of not quite fitting on the furniture?"

"Yes. And I really think they should have discounts for people who can only fit into SUVs and first-class seats on the plane."

Sethie laughs, "That makes it sound like a handicap."

Ben laughs back, "Sometimes it feels like one."

Sethie nods, suddenly serious. She imagines Ben squeezing into spaces that don't quite fit, wishing he were just a little bit smaller. In that respect, she thinks, we're actually quite similar.

Sethie looks at the textbook in Ben's lap; she thinks it's physics. "I thought when you went to college, your textbook days were finally over," Sethie says.

"What'd you think you'd use to study when you got to college?"

Sethie steps inside, shuts the door behind her. "I thought it was, you know, more serious than textbooks. I thought it was novels and short stories and articles."

"Yeah, well," Ben says, standing up. "Physics major. In physics there are always textbooks."

"Oh."

"What are you going to major in?"

Sethie shrugs. "Don't know yet. English, maybe. Or history. Sounds pretty girly next to a physics major."

Ben shakes his head. "I'm minoring in English."

Sethie cocks her head, surprised. "Really?"

"Yeah. American lit, mostly."

"That's what I want to study—the twentieth-century writers. I want to write some enormous thesis proving that even the most wildly different ones have some of the same habits: Hemingway, Faulkner, Steinbeck."

"Have you figured out how you're going to prove it yet?"

"Not yet. But I will."

"I believe you," Ben says seriously. "You seem like the kind of girl who gets done the things she wants to do."

Sethie smiles; she hopes Ben's right. She wanted to be under 111 and now she is at least half of the time. She wanted to get over 2200 on her SATs, and she did. And she wanted Shaw, and she got him; at least she thought she had.

Ben says, "But you gotta throw some women in there: Joan Didion. Katherine Anne Porter. Flannery O'Connor."

"I've never read Flannery O'Connor."

Ben reaches for a book on his desk. "Here," he says. "Read the story called 'Everything That Rises Must Converge.'"

Sethie turns the book over in her hands. "I will."

"Good, 'cause I'll be expecting a full report."

"I wouldn't have pegged you for a literature dork."

"Gotta do something to even out the physics dorkiness."

Sethie smiles. "Maybe I should minor in physics, then—even myself out."

Ben laughs. "Maybe you should." He takes a step toward her. "Can I take your coat?"

"What?" Sethie blinks. "No. I'm not staying long. And it's cold in here anyway." Sethie notices that Ben has the windows open, even though it's December. She's disappointed; she thought being around Ben again would make her warm.

"Well, take a load off anyhow," he says, gesturing to his bed and his desk chair, the only places to sit in his room. She sits on his bed, but gingerly, on the edge of it.

"Ben is short for Benjamin, right?"

Ben nods, sitting down next to her.

"So when they call roll on the first day of class, you have to correct your teachers, right? You have to tell them, No, it's Ben."

Ben laughs. "They don't really call roll in college."

"Maybe just not in the classes that use textbooks," Sethie says, and Ben smiles at her. "I have to correct people all the time. It's not Sarah, or Sarah Beth; it's Sethie, I say. And I get mad at them, at these total strangers for it. You know what I mean?"

"Ben's a lot more obvious of an abbreviation," he says, shaking his head. "But what's wrong with a name that demands a little explanation? Gives it heft, right?"

Sethie considers this. She always thought her name had heft only because of the people who said it. Shaw, with his gravelly opera voice, Janey with her perfect elocution, and now Ben, with his deep giant's voice.

Sethie thinks she might start to cry, right there, right in

front of Ben. She's hungry, and she's cold, and she knows that Janey is waiting to tell her something she really, really doesn't want to hear.

She bites her lip, takes a deep breath, and says, "Are there any good sushi places around here?"

Ben shrugs. "Depends on what you mean by good."

"Good enough will do just fine."

"Then we have places that are good enough."

"You're studying for finals, though, aren't you?"

"Yeah," Ben says, "but a boy's gotta eat."

Sethie grins. "Judging by the size of you, I'm guessing you eat pretty regularly."

Ben laughs.

"Come on, Sarah Beth."

Janey isn't in sight when Ben opens the door. She must be up in Doug's room. Sethie lets Ben go ahead of her on the stairs; he's still taller, even two steps below her, but at least she's closer to meeting his eye.

"Ben," she says, stopping between steps, and he turns back to look at her. "Are things as complicated in college as they are in high school?" She's surprised that she doesn't mind how young the question must make her seem.

Ben cocks his head to the side. "No," he says slowly. "Things are definitely less complicated in college," he says, and Sethie smiles. "But you still gotta use textbooks," he adds, facing forward and continuing down the steps.

**B**EN IS A healthy eater. Sethie had this idea that because he is so tall, he could eat whatever he wanted and not gain weight. He has so much surface area to metabolize it. Surely it takes more calories to take a 6'7" step than to take a 5'4" one. But Ben has miso soup and a vegetable roll, and he barely uses any soy sauce.

Sethie douses each bite with soy sauce. She read somewhere that real anorexics always use lots of salt, lots of mustard, covering their food in strong tastes to trick their bodies into thinking they've eaten more than they have. She likes having this in common with them. When the waiter takes their dishes away, there are splashes of soy sauce all over Sethie's side of the table and her cloth napkin has practically turned from white to brown. It looks, Sethie thinks after they get up and she sees it left behind on the white tablecloth, like a used tourniquet, covered in blood that has dried and turned brown.

Ben is walking slowly, but his legs are so long that Sethie

still feels like they are rushing, and the last thing she wants is to rush back to his fraternity house. She considers hailing a cab then and there, going straight home without seeing Janey. Ben said there was no way Janey was sleeping with Shaw; Janey and Doug have fallen so hard for each other, he said. But Sethie countered that they might have been hooking up before Janey and Doug met. Maybe Janey and Shaw have been keeping it all a secret from her, the silly girl who thought she had a boyfriend when she really just had a fuck buddy. She can't quite believe that she's admitted all of this to Ben. She knows what a fool it makes her, what a little girl she has been. Someone naive enough to think that all that sex translated into a real relationship. But Ben didn't seem to think she was immature. If anything, Ben said, that meant her idea of interpersonal relations was more adult than Shaw's. But Sethie knows he was just being nice. Sethie knows that no guy would want a girl like her now. A girl who's been humiliated, a girl who completely misunderstood the rules of sleeping with the boy with whom she'd been sleeping. For the first time, tonight, she said out loud that she was in love with Shaw. She never said it before, certainly never thought she would say it to Shaw. And now she's said it to this other boy whom she really doesn't know at all.

When she said it, Ben shrugged. At first, Sethie thought he was shrugging off her feelings, like they weren't real; she was only in high school, what did she know about love? She thought he was shrugging because an older girl would not have misread the signs; an older girl would have known better than to fall in love with Shaw, would have known better than to believe she had a boyfriend, would have known better than to believe he probably loved her too in some hidden, unarticulated way.

But instead, Ben said, "We really can't help who we fall for."

"Whom," Sethie corrected. "Whom we fall for." And Sethie found she was smiling when she should have been embarrassed, making fun of Ben for his grammar and feeling good, because she knew that she was a smart girl, when she had been feeling so stupid just a second ago.

"Whom," Ben repeated. "You're the only person I've ever met who knows when to use which words." He says it like it's a good thing.

And now they're walking back to the frat house, and Sethie is surprised to find that she's holding Ben's hand. She just reached out and took it, just like that, like it was the most natural thing in the world. Exactly the way she was always too scared to take Shaw's hand. And she feels better, braver, holding Ben's hand.

They stop in his room on their way up to Doug's. Ben scribbles something on a pad on his desk, rips off the paper.

"This is my number," he says. "Call me any time things seem a little too complicated."

Ben is standing beside her when she knocks on Doug's door. Janey is lying in Doug's bed, but she sits up straight when she sees Sethie.

"I didn't know you were still here."

"I wasn't for a while. We went out to dinner."

Janey smiles. "That's nice."

Sethie thinks that in spite of everything else, Janey is still holding out hope that Sethie and Ben will get together just like she and Doug did.

"We were just killing time," Sethie adds quickly, and Janey nods.

"Doug had to go to the library. He has finals next week."

"I know. Ben does too."

From behind Sethie, Ben says, "Actually, I better get back to studying too. You girls okay to let yourselves out?"

They both nod, and Ben closes Doug's door behind him.

"It's strange to be in here without Doug here," Sethie says finally.

"I'm getting used to it," Janey says.

"I thought you must be sleeping with Shaw," Sethie says. "But Ben said you would never cheat on Doug."

Janey shakes her head. "I think we're in love," she says.

"You do?"

Janey smiles. "Yeah. We've been talking about it. We keep saying we're almost in love."

"There are steps?"

Janey shrugs. "I guess for us there are. I'm going home with him over break."

"Where does he live?"

"Virginia."

"Oh, right. I forgot."

Sethie sits down on the couch now, across from Janey. Janey says *Virginia* like it's a magical place, exotic and new. And for all Sethie knows, it is. Virginia is the land of Thomas Jefferson and Dave Matthews. An older boy from Virginia is very different from a boy who's a month younger than you and lives just a couple of blocks away. Apparently a boy from Virginia can tell you not only that he loves you but even talk about the process of falling for you.

"Nice Southern boy," Sethie says, and Janey smiles again.

"I know. Sometimes, when he's on the phone with his parents, a little bit of a Southern accent comes out."

"So you're not sleeping with Shaw."

"No!"

"And you didn't used to be?"

"No."

Sethie looks at the ceiling, her vision blurred by the beginning of tears in her eyes. She can't imagine what secret Janey and Shaw could have, other than that. But she's not crying because she's sad; she's crying because she is still missing Shaw; even now, she wishes he were here and she could curl up against him.

"Sethie, he told me that you guys were just friends who hooked up from time to time. He told me that last year, whenever it started. And I didn't meet you until September, and I had no idea what you were like."

"What difference does that make?"

"Because I should have told you the minute I met you and wanted to be your friend. And I certainly should have told you when you called Shaw your boyfriend last week.

But I thought I owed something to Shaw, because he was my friend first."

"Owed him something?"

"You know, like my loyalty. Like I should give him the chance to tell you himself, before I did."

"The chance to tell me himself?"

Janey looks down at Doug's blankets. "He sleeps around. With girls in our class." Sethie nods. She tries to imagine when he sees these other girls; maybe he squeezes it in between classes. Maybe he and the girls sneak down to the school basement, the school darkroom, the bottoms of the stairwells. Maybe they meet up before school in the morning, secret trysts before breakfast. She thinks it can't have begun before they slept together; they were each other's firsts.

Janey says, "And now there's some girl here at Columbia."

Sethie remembers the girl who sat next to Shaw on the couch on Saturday night. She remembers the way Shaw didn't seem to want her around that night. She remembers how he left without her.

"That's what we were fighting about when you saw us this afternoon. I wanted him to tell you himself, but he didn't think he had to."

"Because he thinks we're just fuck buddies," Sethie supplies.

"I hate that phrase," Janey says.

Sethie shrugs. She never liked it either, but then she

never thought that it reflected what she was. "Friends with benefits?" she offers as an alternative, and Janey shrugs.

"I guess. He didn't give it a name." Janey pulls Doug's blankets taut across her lap. "So maybe I was feeling guilty; maybe I was hoping that if I set you up with Ben, the whole Shaw thing just wouldn't matter anymore."

"Apparently it didn't matter."

"It mattered to you."

Sethie looks at the ceiling. "I think I want to go home."

"Okay," Janey says, swinging her legs over the side of Doug's bed. "I'll come with you."

Sethie shakes her head. "No. No. It's not one in the morning or anything. I can walk myself out." And she turns around and runs down the stairs, taking them two at a time, like a little kid who can't wait to get downstairs on Christmas morning to see what Santa has brought her. On the sidewalk, she holds her left wrist in her right hand, and presses the fingers of her left hand to her mouth, walking as fast as she can. She lets go of her wrist to hail a cab, and when she slams the cab door behind her, Sethie is thinking two things: Oh God, I miss Shaw, and I hope this cab gets me home in time.

**HOME IN TIME** means in time to throw up her dinner. It's been more than an hour since she finished her meal and since then she's skipped down stairs and run to a cab, moves that surely have made her metabolism start digesting. It's funny to her that she's racing her metabolism, the very thing whose slowness makes her need to throw up in the first place.

In the taxi, she runs the numbers in her head. Bagel with mustard for lunch. Edamame. Miso soup. Four pieces of sushi. Soy sauce. She guesses the calories: 500 plus 100 plus 200 plus 400. Only 1200. She's never thrown up on only 1200. She's never thrown up when she ate exactly what she had planned to. But she knows that she wants to tonight. She slams her bathroom door behind her and curls her body over the toilet; she throws up until her stomach hurts and there are pieces of raw fish underneath her fingernails. She throws up until she can't tell whether she's crying because Shaw slept with other girls, because Janey knew and didn't tell her, or because of the way she's scratched her throat raw. Maybe she's crying because she hates throwing up; a bulimic, Sethie thinks bitterly, is just an anorexic who isn't trying hard enough, and I'm not even a real bulimic. When she pulls her hair into a ponytail afterward, she can see flecks of food shining against her scalp. But she can't wash her hair now, because she's already washed her hair once today and she knows that you're not supposed to wash your hair twice on the same day. Janey doesn't even wash her hair every day because her hairdresser says that's so much better for her scalp. Sethie decides that it would be better for her hair if she just got into bed with it dirty; she can wash it, and her pillowcases, in the morning.

Rebecca isn't home, so Sethie puts on a tight tank top so that she will feel and see all the weight she still should lose; she would never wear something so tight when there was a chance Rebecca might see her. Alone, she will see a reminder of her fat in every reflective surface: the mirror in the bathroom, the windows of her bedroom, even the shining wood floors. The fabric of the shirt will always be touching her skin, unlike the loose, flowy tops she usually favors, so she will always feel her fat.

Sethie doesn't answer the phone when it rings; it can only be Janey checking up on her, and she doesn't want to talk to Janey. Or maybe it's Shaw, Shaw who doesn't know what Sethie's been told, and he's calling to come over for what Sethie now understands is only a booty call. Sethie keeps her bedroom door shut and the phone shoved under her pillow; if her mother comes home, she won't be able to hear the phone ring and wonder why Sethie isn't answering it.

Sethie is so hot that she can't sleep. Every piece of her body is sticky, her fingers smell like vomit, her hairline is covered in sweat. When she lies on her side, she can feel her thighs rubbing together, and when she shifts, it feels like moist cold cuts being pulled apart.

She opens the window; it's December out, it should be cool. She kicks the blanket to the foot of the bed, then gets up and rearranges it so that it's folded neatly on the floor. She pulls the sheets around her only so that she can put them in between all the parts of her that stick; between her knees and ankles, her arms and the sides of her torso. Her warm tears only make her hotter. She takes a Valium to fall asleep. Janey gave her a handful weeks ago, her mother's prescription. They didn't even have to sneak it out of the medicine cabinet, since Janey's parents are never home anyway.

This hot, Sethie can't even pretend that the pillow where she rests her head is Shaw's chest; if Shaw were here, she'd never be so warm.

Sethie is happy to have school in the morning. She's happy that she doesn't go to the same school as Shaw and Janey, and she's happy that finals are coming up and she has so much work to do. She's even happy that she has a school uniform, because she honestly doesn't think she could decide so much as what to wear anymore.

And after school, she still doesn't answer her phone. She can see that the battery is almost dead, but she decides not to charge it. She sits on the floor of her room and she studies, and she takes another Valium to fall asleep, and she drinks cold water, but she still feels hot.

Sethie hasn't gone to the bathroom in five days. She's peed, of course, but she hasn't had a bowel movement in five days. She began recording them in her food journal almost a month ago: *December 3rd, 4 p.m.: half a bagel with peanut butter for lunch, shat, three pieces of cinnamon Trident during class.* But now, she hasn't gone for days. She feels bloated; she knows that if she could just shit, she would lose more weight. Tonight, finally, she goes; she has terrible diarrhea. On the toilet, she doubles over so that her chest is resting on her thighs. She wishes she had a clock in her bathroom, so that she would know how long she's been going for. She wonders if her stomach has ever hurt this much; she wonders which food it was that triggered this. Some unwashed lettuce in the salad she had for lunch, perhaps, or bad fish in her sushi last night (some of it must have stayed down). In the toilet, she can see whole pieces of the food she ate, completely undigested. In her journal she writes: *Shitty shits. Finally.*

§ § §

On Thursday, Shaw is waiting for her after school. Sethie is wearing her coat unbuttoned; her body still can't get cool.

"Hey, kiddo," he says, and he turns on his heel in the direction of Sethie's apartment. Sethie follows him.

"I brought you some hot chocolate," Shaw says, pressing a cup into Sethie's hands. Some of the drink spills out of the cup onto her fingers. It's already cold from having been held by Shaw, but Sethie doesn't mind. Maybe it will cool her off.

"Why?" Sethie asks.

"You're always cold," Shaw answers, shrugging. "And anyway, you never eat enough."

Sethie smiles. That's right, she thinks, I barely eat anything at all. But she sips the hot chocolate, even though Shaw probably doesn't know that you're supposed to order it with skim milk, and you should never get whipped cream. She sips it because Shaw's given it to her, and she sips it because she's only had coffee and a low-fat granola bar so far today; she honestly can't seem to stop herself from sipping it.

"I think your phone is broken," Shaw says as they walk.

"Yeah," Sethie says. "It might be." Sethie likes the idea that Shaw has been trying to call her. And Sethie follows him into the vacant apartment like nothing has changed.

"I heard they rented this place," she says when he passes her the joint.

"Thought they never would."

"Me too."

Shaw takes a long hit and says, "Listen, Sethie, I know Janey told you about Anna."

Sethie shakes her head. "Anna?" The name sounds familiar in Shaw's voice.

"Janey told me she told you. You met her, remember? At the frat house."

Sethie thinks. "I'm not sure," she says finally.

"Listen, I know it's silly, but I think I really like her."

Sethie wonders why he keeps beginning sentences with the word *listen*. She's listening as hard as she can.

"So, listen, I think we have to stop that part of our friendship for now."

Sethie wishes she weren't stoned. She stands up.

"There's no reason to get upset," Shaw says.

"I'm not upset."

Shaw reaches up for her hand, and pulls her down into his lap. "I didn't think things were going to get serious with her. I thought it would be like us, but she's not that kind of girl."

Sethie settles into Shaw's lap. She's wondering what kind of girl that means she is. Shaw is kissing her neck.

"How about one last time?"

"Hmmm?" Sethie asks, but he kisses her again, and seems to have interpreted her "Hmmm" for "Mmmm." His cold fingers are reaching under her tights, and somehow that sensation seems louder than anything he's said. She lies down underneath him and closes her eyes. She thinks he said something about this being the last time. She thinks that she will finally be cool now, with Shaw's torso pressed against hers. She thinks that she will miss this. She's not sure when she begins to cry, but Shaw doesn't know, because he can't see her face. Shaw's head is to the left of hers, his chin hovering over her shoulder.

When it's over, he kisses her face where she's been crying, and she doesn't understand why he's being so tender. She doesn't understand anything, least of all why she's naked on the floor. Her hips are sore from where Shaw's hip bones pressed into them, but she doesn't mind, because that means she's skinny today.

"I better get dressed," Shaw says. Sethie looks up at him. He's not really undressed, she thinks. His shirt is still on and his pants are down around his ankles. Only one of his shoes is off.

"I'm glad we did this. Kinda like saying good-bye to the physical part of our friendship."

Sethie nods.

"Anna could tell when she saw you at the frat house the other night. She said enough was enough. She wants to really be together."

Sethie nods. She thinks that Shaw is the only high school boy she knows who could get a college girl.

"So I thought, okay, this chick is worth it. I mean," he says, buckling his belt, "she's the kind of girl that you fall in love with, right?"

"I only met her for a second," Sethie says. She remembers having met Anna now; she'd thought Anna was with Jeff Cooper. Anna had long brown hair with just a little bit of a wave to it, and had been wearing a red top that showed off her flat stomach.

"Just wait. You'll see—she's really special."

More special than I am, apparently, Sethie thinks but does not say. Sethie wonders if he uses condoms with Anna.

"I'm going home with her over the break. Her family lives in Palm Beach."

Shaw kisses her on the cheek to say good-bye, just like he says good-bye to Janey, when she's standing up and fully dressed. When he closes the door, Sethie thinks, Well, I guess they rented this place at the perfect time.

**S** ETHIE SPENDS THE weekend studying. These are her senior year finals, after all, the grades that colleges will look at. She stays up late to reread *What Maisie Knew* cover to cover for her English exam, even though really she's just procrastinating having to study calculus. She stops reading when she notices the picture frames on her windowsill are crooked, and she has to get up to straighten them. She takes Valium to sleep, because it's perfectly sensible to take Valium to sleep, perfectly sensible to need help relaxing when finals are coming. It's perfectly normal to be so busy that you don't have time to eat. Perfectly normal that her phone never rings, not because she's let the battery die, but because, of course, all of her friends are busy studying too. Perfectly normal that she keeps her bedroom door tightly closed and comes out only to go to the bathroom. Rebecca needn't wonder why she's staying home every night; she can, Sethie thinks, be grateful to have such a conscientious, ambitious child.

Janey shows up the evening after Sethie has taken her last final: essay questions on American history; Sethie wrote about black soldiers during the Civil War. Sethie thinks that she's been taught the same history over and over but with different twists. When we were seven, they taught us that slavery didn't exist in America after the Civil War. At seventeen, we have a teacher who tells us that slavery still hasn't ended; it's just not quite so visible, not quite so clear.

Janey eyes Sethie carefully as she stands in her doorway. Sethie wonders what she's looking at so closely. This morning, Sethie put on makeup, though it's smudged now. After finals, they took photos of all of the different clubs for the yearbook. Sethie was in two; one for the yearbook editorial staff, and one for the White Environmental Action Club, the acronym for which is WEAC, which amuses all the members, since the club doesn't really do anything or represent any actions, other than the action of allowing its members to list it on their college applications.

Sethie's been in the club since seventh grade. Then she wanted to make a difference; she started a campaign for recycling bins to be placed on every floor and next to the copy machines in the library. Everyone acted like it was such a big deal. The teachers were proud of her, and the headmistress even spoke about it at that year's graduation ceremonies. But after a while, Sethie noticed that people still threw recyclables in the trash cans, or they threw the wrong things into the recycling bins, like soda cans into the paper bins and paper into the bins for plastics. It really hadn't made any difference at all. But they did make her the president of WEAC this year, maybe, Sethie thinks, as an homage to her seventh-grade activism. So this afternoon, she had to sit in the center of the picture, even though she'd have much rather been in the back; being behind other girls would have covered up the fat around her belly.

Worse, though, was the yearbook editorial picture. Sethie felt like an imposter there. Everyone looked at her like they knew why she'd stopped going to meetings, and good riddance too. Who wants a managing editor who can't even be responsible enough to keep from eating pizza at our meetings, their looks seemed to say. That girl can't possibly be responsible enough to put a yearbook together.

"You're staring at me," Sethie mumbles to Janey finally. She is holding open her front door; only halfway, so that Janey knows she is not invited in.

"What?" Janey asks. "I didn't hear you."

"Nothing."

Janey blinks. "You're not answering your phone."

Sethie shrugs.

"You look like hell," Janey adds.

"Well, you know, finals."

"I had my English final yesterday."

"Oh?" Sethie stops herself from asking how it went.

"I think I did okay. Well, I mean. Thanks to you."

Sethie shrugs. She had liked helping Janey with English. It made her feel good.

Janey says, "I know you're mad at me."

Sethie shrugs again. She's not sure what she is, other than hungry.

"I should have told you sooner. About Shaw, I mean. I just felt this loyalty to him. Like, he was my friend first or something."

All Sethie can think to say is "You said that already."

Janey asks if she can come in.

"Why?" Sethie says, and Janey's face crumples. Janey is wearing a turtleneck sweater, but Sethie imagines that if she could see her collarbone now, it would be dull and dry.

"Sethie, you'll be my friend last, that's what I wanted to say. My loyalty is to you, and he hurt you."

Sethie shrugs. "He didn't hurt me. I just misunderstood."

"He misrepresented."

"No, he didn't. He never called me his girlfriend. It wasn't his fault."

"It wasn't yours."

"I really don't want to talk about this, okay?"

"Okay."

"I don't really want to talk at all."

"Okay."

"Okay."

"But if you change your mind"—Janey reaches into her pocket and offers Sethie a slip of paper—"this is the number where I'm staying in Virginia. Doug's parents' place. He said I might not have cell service there."

Sethie takes the number and puts it in her own jeans pocket. She's not quite sure what to do with it.

"We're leaving tomorrow morning."

Sethie nods. Tomorrow is Christmas Eve.

"Merry Christmas," Janey says.

"Okay." Sethie considers making a joke about being Jewish, but it seems like it would take too much effort.

"I'd say Happy New Year too, but we'll talk before then." Sethie shrugs. "Sure."

"Okay." Janey turns around and presses the button for the elevator. Sethie thinks that she would have better believed that Janey wanted to come in if she'd unzipped her winter coat. But then, Sethie made it clear that she wasn't exactly welcome.

**L**ATER, SETHIE FINDS another piece of paper, with another phone number. She puts it next to her phone, on her nightstand. She hates the furniture in her room; white wicker, left over from a phase she went through when she was ten and wanted everything to be white. White wicker dresser and desk, white bedspread. Rebecca says there's no point in replacing anything, with Sethie going away to school next year.

Sethie glances at the paper on her nightstand as she changes into her pajamas and gets her bottle of water. She takes a vitamin called chromium picolinate before she begins to drink, because one of the girls at school said it makes you lose weight.

By the time she picks up her phone to dial the number, she's already memorized it. She slips the paper into her desk drawer. She plugs her phone into its charger so that it will have the power it needs for one call. She stretches the cord to stand in the center of the room and holds her phone out in front of her, presses the numbers. Ben picks up on the second ring.

"I read 'Everything That Rises Must Converge,'" Sethie says instead of hello. "I should have been studying, but I read your story instead." Sethie steps over to her bed and sits up tall in the center of it, her legs crossed underneath her.

"It's not my story."

"It is as far as I'm concerned."

Sethie thinks Ben is smiling now. "Well, what did you think?"

Sethie takes a deep breath before answering. "I loved it. The hat."

"Yeah."

"And the mom."

"I know."

"Brilliant."

"Positively."

"If I get into Columbia, you're going to have to tell me which class it was that you read that in. I want a teacher to help me figure out what it all means."

Ben laughs. "When you get into Columbia, I will be happy to guide you in your course selection."

"Hey, I'm perfectly capable of picking my classes."

"I'm sure you are. I'm just also perfectly capable of helping."

Sethie smiles. She uncrosses her legs.

"I've done two bad things," she says slowly. "But I can't seem to decide which one to tell you first."

"Is one worse than the other?"

Sethie closes her eyes.

"Yes."

"Then tell me in order of badness."

"I'm not honestly sure which one is the worst."

"Hey, at least you know they were bad. That's half the battle."

"All right, G.I. Joe."

"Tell me both at once, and I'll figure out which one was worse."

"I sent Janey away." Sethie's shoulders slump as she says it. She makes herself sit up straight again; sitting up straight is good exercise for your abs.

"What do you mean you sent her away? She's going away, with Doug."

"I don't mean I sent her to Virginia, numnuts."

"Dude, you know nothing about my nuts," Ben says, and Sethie giggles.

"I sent her away from my door. She came over to talk to me, to check up on me I think, but I sent her away."

"Why?"

"Well, I'm angry at her."

"Why?"

"She should have told me about Shaw sooner." Sethie assumes he knows what she's talking about.

"Maybe she should have."

"And maybe she only came over here because she was feeling guilty for not having told me sooner and wanted to make sure I wasn't, like, slitting my wrists over it or something."

"Were you?"

"No."

"Well, that's a good first step."

"Thanks, I worked hard on it." Sethie smiles; even now, she is flirting with Ben. The retorts come so easily; that was never the case with Shaw. She was always scared to irritate Shaw.

Ben says, "So you sent her away, because she waited too long to tell you, exposing you to all kinds of heartbreak and humiliation? Even though, when she realized how wrong she was, she felt bad about it, and wanted to make sure you were okay?"

Sethie considers this. "I guess not."

"That's not why you sent her away?"

"No."

"Then why?"

Sethie tries to take a deep breath around the lump that's formed in her throat. "I think I was embarrassed."

"Embarrassed?"

"Yeah. Embarrassed. That I fell for Shaw, that everyone knew he was sleeping around, that I was so stupid." Sethie can hardly believe the words can make their way past the lump.

"That's what happens when you're in love. That's where that whole 'love is blind' thing came from."

"I thought that meant that when you're in love, the

person you love becomes more good-looking to you. That you can't see if they, you know, gain weight."

At least Sethie certainly hopes that's what it means, so that someday maybe there will be one less thing to scare her about gaining weight.

Ben says, "That too. But also that you can be totally blindsided by the person you're in love with."

"I don't think that's what they meant."

"Well, that's because you're not up on my modern, hip interpretation. You have nothing to be embarrassed about."

Sethie closes her eyes. "Well, there's something else. The other reason I sent Janey away."

"Why's that?"

"Because I knew if she came in I would probably tell her the second bad thing that I did."

"What's the second bad thing?"

Sethie keeps her eyes shut. "I'm not sure I can say it out loud."

"Try saying it like it's about someone else."

Sethie opens her eyes. She lies down so that her feet are on her pillows. Even though she's washed her sheets since the last time Shaw was here, she believes that the pillow-cases still smell like him.

"Someone who slept with the guy she thought was her boyfriend but discovered he was really only using her for sex and probably also for a place to smoke pot? Someone who slept with him while he told her about his new girl-friend who is, apparently, the kind of girl that he could really fall in love with?"

Sethie is surprised to have said all of that, surprised at the ease with which the words came out of her mouth. Ben was right; saying it about someone else did make it easier. She said it, and she's not even crying. In a minute, she will even be laughing.

"Jeez," Ben says. "That girl has issues."

"Tell me about it," Sethie says, and now she laughs. She's grateful Ben made a joke; it's a relief to be a punch line, even if it is a punch line about being a basket case.

"Keep me the hell away from a chick like that," Ben continues, and Sethie stops laughing. Maybe she had no business confiding all of this in Ben.

"Sethie?" Ben says when he hears how quiet she's gotten.

"Yeah?" She knows when she speaks, her voice sounds small. She imagines that when someone's as tall as Ben is, even his voice is bigger.

"I don't think you really are a girl like that. I think you only were for a second there, or a few months there. But I don't think that's who you really are."

Sethie quietly says, "Who do you think I really am?" But she doesn't intend for Ben to answer; she doesn't even intend for him to hear.

"You're the only girl I ever met who understood that it's not so great, being this size. And you're the only girl I ever met who wants to write a paper about Ernest Hemingway."

Sethie likes the girl Ben thinks she is. She likes who she is on the phone with Ben, just like she liked who she was at dinner with him, and on the couch beside him. She is brazen and brash, flirty and opinionated. She isn't a girl who curls over toilets and counts calories. This girl is so much easier than that. By the end of this phone call, this girl nicknames Ben "the Giant" without even worrying that it might offend him.

Ben says, "As long as you don't say 'jolly green.' "

"Nah," Sethie says. "That's not you. You're the friendly giant, like in *The Princess Bride*. You look scary, but you're the one who really rescues everyone in the end."

"I never saw that movie."

"You're kidding. It's my favorite. I practically burned a hole in my copy, I watched it so many times."

"And you just gave away the ending."

Sethie laughs. "Don't worry. I really didn't. We'll watch it sometime, and I'll prove it to you."

"All right then, it's a date. After the break."

"Okay," Sethie says. "After the break."

"And Sethie?"

"Yeah?"

"I figured out which one of the two bad things you did was worse."

"Oh yeah, how long did that take you?"

"I knew the answer even before you told me number two. It was sending Janey away. And you know it, too."

Sethie doesn't say anything.

"Okay, well, till after the break, then."

"Right, after the break."

"You take care of yourself while I'm gone."

"You too. I mean, while you're gone. Stay warm up there."

"Dude, up there is my only chance to cool off."

Sethie smiles, and says good night and Happy New Year. When she hangs up, she unplugs her phone so that the battery will die again. Now that Ben is off to Vermont, there honestly isn't anyone left she wants to talk to.

**T**WO DAYS AFTER Janey leaves, Sethie begins to leave all the windows open in her room. A cold snap has hit New York City, and Sethie likes the sound of that; a snap is something sharp, like breaking open peas that have soaked in water until they're turgid. Cold like a snap of the fingers that can get your attention, stop you from what you are doing, or send you on your way. When she drinks her water, Sethie fills the bottle with ice cubes. She has been too warm for the last few days—days spent without Shaw. Sethie thinks that if she can just get cold enough, it will feel like Shaw is with her.

She charges her phone. Maybe Shaw has been trying to call; after all, he says they're still friends. He says they always have been. But when the phone rings, it's never Shaw, and Sethie lets it go to voice mail. Every phone call is from Janey.

Sethie checks her voice mail after each call.

"Hi Sethie, just wanted to wish you Merry Christmas."

"Hi Sethie, I miss you. It's freezing in Virginia. I thought the South was supposed to be warm!"

"Sethie, I'm getting a little worried. Call me back at Doug's house, please, just to tell me you're okay. Or if you don't want to talk to me, leave me a message at home that you're okay, and I'll get it when I check my messages. Please, Sethie, I miss you."

Sethie deletes the new messages; she hears the words Janey's saying, but she doesn't want to listen. There are saved messages from Shaw in her voice mail box. She plays them a few times, and it feels like she's hearing his growling voice through her belly instead of through her ears.

§ § §

Five days after Janey leaves, Sethie is sick of being cold and sick of waiting for Shaw. She shuts the windows and turns the heat as high as it goes, burning her hand on the old radiator. I should be hot, Sethie thinks. I should not be trying to feel Shaw here, to imitate his touch, to re-create his kisses by sucking on ice cubes. I should not be inviting him in through the open windows; I should be keeping him out behind locked doors. She will sweat him out. She layers on sweatpants and a sweatshirt, even a hat and scarf. She tells herself that Shaw is in the sweat leaving her body. And she tells herself the harder she sweats, the more weight she will lose—an added bonus.

Sethie lets the phone battery run out again so that even if Shaw does call, she won't be tempted to talk to him. It's bad enough, she thinks, that there's all this extra flesh making me fat, but it's also extra flesh that Shaw touched, extra flesh that misses him now. She is sure, though she only saw her for a second, that Shaw's new girlfriend is skinny and flat and that her stomach curls into a C when she slouches. Sethie corrects herself; Anna is not his "new" girlfriend. She can only be new if Sethie was old, and Sethie was never his. Or he was never hers. She can't remember which one she's upset about. It's so confusing, to feel that she's been dumped even though it's perfectly clear to everyone else, apparently, that she and Shaw were never a couple to begin with.

Sethie can't believe just how alone she is; a month ago, she imagined spending Christmas with Shaw, or at least with Janey. Now they're each with their respective significant others. Sethie gnaws on the word *significant* like it's a piece of gum.

She decides to clean out her desk. She empties each of the five drawers completely and spreads the contents on the floor around her. She can't think what to throw away, so she arranges everything into piles and places each pile back into the drawers. She can imagine Shaw sitting on her bed while she cleans; he would laugh over her inability to throw anything away. He would have told her to get stoned before cleaning. Sethie climbs into her bed; she sleeps as much as she can. She doesn't bother getting dressed; she stays in her pajamas so that she can always get into bed and try to sleep. She can't eat in her sleep. And when she sleeps, she isn't hungry.

Eight days after Janey leaves, Sethie walks into the kitchen. It is midday on New Year's Eve, and Sethie has no plans to go out. She has decided to take some more of Janey's mother's Valium and go to sleep early. Sethie has not left the house since she took her last final, the day before Christmas Eve, the day before Janey left for Virginia and Shaw left for Florida and Ben left for Vermont. The day before everyone left her here, leaving her no choice but to go into the kitchen and run her fingers over her mother's knives.

It's not that she wants something sharp. A dull knife will do just fine. A dinner knife; sharper than a butter knife, but not as sharp as a steak knife. The knife she is most familiar with; the one she uses to cut up pieces of white-meat-only chicken, to scrape peanut butter thin across wheat toast, to peel the skin off of apples.

When she was little, Sethie always imagined what it would be like not to be Jewish, to have a house filled with lights and presents at Christmastime. A tree and a fire and a Christmas Eve dinner and a big breakfast on Christmas Day. The kitchen filled with leftovers all through winter break. Now, she is grateful to be Jewish. There are no leftovers in her kitchen to tempt her. Only some old cheese and dry pasta, only frozen chicken cutlets and Diet Coke. And dinner knives.

Sethie's mother is in her bedroom; she has plans tonight. She's already getting ready. A friend of hers is having a dinner party. She invited Sethie to come, but Sethie laughed. Staying at home alone still seems like something better to do than going with her mother to a party.

She brings one of the knives into her bedroom and slides it between her mattress and box spring. She doesn't know why she feels she needs to hide it well. Her mother will only pop her head in before leaving; under the covers or in the closet would have served just as well.

Sethie waits until her mother leaves, and then she takes off all of her clothes and lies on the hardwood floor. She repeats her old ritual of going over her body with a hand mirror, but this time, she uses the knife. She sits up to run it over her legs, holding it above her skin but so close that she can feel the cool of the metal pricking the hair on her legs, which she hasn't shaved for days, since she hasn't bathed for days.

Sweating him out hasn't worked. She still misses Shaw. Throwing up hasn't worked. She still feels fat. It seems the only thing left is to cut off the fat and to scrape away at the layers of skin that Shaw touched, the layers of skin that remember how his touch felt. She will make herself free of fat; she will make herself clean of Shaw.

Sethie's shoulder blades press into the floor. The blade finds its way to her hip bone. Sethie's favorite part, the part where the bone protrudes: the skinniest place on her body. She makes a light scratch, just enough to turn the skin beneath it white. Then presses just a little bit harder, so the skin begins to turn red. She feels like a creature out of a fairy tale: a girl who discovers that her bones are really made out of stone, that her skin is really as fragile as glass, that her hair is brittle as straw, that her tears have dried up so that she cries only salt. Maybe that's why it doesn't hurt when she presses hard enough to begin bleeding: it doesn't hurt, because she isn't real anymore.

# 19.

SCHOOL BEGINS ON a Monday, almost a week after New Year's Eve, and on Sunday, Sethie's mother knocks on Sethie's door. Sethie is lying in bed; her mother doesn't wait for a response to her knock before she sticks her head into the room. Sethie looks at her mother's bare feet. She thinks about her eighth-grade health teacher, who brought a Barbie into class and said that there was no way that, were Barbie life-size, such small feet could support her body. Even then, Sethie thought: you've obviously never met my mother.

"How about brunch?" Rebecca says.

"I'm not really awake yet, Mom," Sethie says.

"I'll wait," Rebecca replies, and Sethie rolls over, away from her, facing the wall.

"Okay, but you might have to wait a long time. I'm not going to waste the last day before school starts by getting out of bed early."

She says it like a regular bratty teenager, she says it like she really is concerned about her last day to sleep late and stay in bed all day. But the truth is that, having barely left the house for two weeks, Sethie doesn't quite remember the steps to getting up, getting ready, getting dressed, and she wants to give herself some extra time to remember them. Her hair is so greasy, she thinks, she will have to shampoo it at least three times. But then she remembers that Janey's hairdresser says you should let your hair get greasy in between shampoos anyway.

Sethie swings her legs over her bed and plants her bare feet on the floor. This part, she thinks, is easy. I've gotten out of bed plenty of times since Janey left: to go to the bathroom, to walk into the kitchen, to search for the remote control when it fell under the bed. But she hasn't changed her clothes since New Year's Eve. She shivers when she lifts her T-shirt over her head. Not because she's cold, but because she is not used to her own bare skin. Being naked feels strange, after so many days in the same clothes.

In the shower, Sethie wraps her arms around herself, folding one so that it lies across her stomach and the other so that it lies across her back. She is thin enough that she can grab her opposite elbows. She pulls her fingers across her belly, pressing against her skin. She can barely even grab her belly fat. Her fingers stop at the scab on her hip. She picks at it so that it bleeds again, and then she rubs soap into it so that it hurts. It begins at her hip bone and snakes onto her belly. It's beginning to scar.

The cut would not have left a scar, Sethie thinks, if she'd only let it alone. It wasn't such a deep cut, though she did press the knife deeper as she moved down toward her belly, down to the fatter place. But as it began to heal, Sethie couldn't stop picking at it, pressing on it. There's a name for it, she thinks: to worry a wound. That's what she did. She didn't let it heal; she made it bleed again instead. But she likes knowing that she will have a scar; like how some people get tattoos to remember the important moments in their lives.

She doesn't bother blow-drying her hair; she doesn't put on makeup. She chooses sweatpants, and she pulls the drawstring waist tight so that it rubs against her scabs, opening them again as she walks, sits down, stands up. Her mother suggests a nice restaurant about eight blocks from their house, and Sethie wonders how many calories she can burn off in the walk to and from the restaurant. She wonders why her mother is choosing such a nice place when Sethie's dressed the way she is. She winds a scarf tightly around her neck and shoves a hat over her wet hair. She doesn't mind that she'll be cold on the walk to the restaurant, though; shivering burns calories, too.

Her mother's coat is black and fitted. Sethie feels like a little girl next to her; her coat is baggy, and she knows that without makeup, she probably looks even younger than she is. The doormen on Park Avenue tip their hats at Rebecca; a man in a tie doesn't even pretend not to stare at her as he walks past. Rebecca takes it all in stride. Sethie looks at her feet as they walk. None of them are looking at her, not the way she looks now. But she can remember, only a year or two ago, when the men began looking at her more than they did her mother. She can remember feeling both triumphant and guilty.

When they sit down, the waiter places a large basket of bread in front of them. Her mother reaches for a piece of baguette and rubs butter all over it. Sethie reaches for the cinnamon raisin bread with walnuts. It used to be her favorite; she used to ask her mother to take her to this restaurant just for this bread. Maybe that's why her mother suggested this place; maybe she remembered that it used to be Sethie's favorite. She can't possibly know that now Sethie would never choose a place with bread like this.

But she can't seem to stop her fingers from placing the bread on her plate, from ripping it into smaller pieces, from wrapping around the butter knife, and spreading the butter across the bread. She can't stop her hands from bringing the bread into her mouth, her jaw from chewing it, her throat from swallowing it, her stomach from accepting it.

It's okay, she thinks, I can throw it up later. She looks down at her hands, and her stomach, and says silently, "Eat all you want, kids."

"Are you excited to go back to school?" Sethie's mother asks.

"Huh?" Sethie had almost forgotten her mother was there, forgotten anyone was there, other than the bread.

"Are you excited to go back to school?" Rebecca repeats.

"Oh, sure. I don't know. My grades don't really matter anymore." Sethie butters another piece of bread, puts it in her mouth, reaches into the bread basket for more.

"Everything's already gone off to colleges," she explains.

"Right." Rebecca chews her own piece of bread. "Well, I'm sure you'll be happy to have your friends back in town."

Sethie shrugs. I must have told Rebecca, she thinks, that my friends were all out of town, so that she wouldn't think it was odd when I barely left the house for two straight weeks. Sethie doesn't remember, but that sounds right.

When the waiter takes their orders, Sethie orders an omelet with cheese. She doesn't even bother specifying egg whites only; it doesn't matter since she's going to throw it all up later. Her mother asks her more about going back to school, but Sethie's too distracted to answer more than monosyllabically; she's thinking about getting back to the apartment in time to throw up. After brunch, Sethie's mother offers to take Sethie shopping, but Sethie turns her down. So they head off in opposite directions; Sethie's mother toward Bloomingdale's and Sethie toward their apartment. She walks slowly, making as little effort as possible. She doesn't want her body to begin metabolizing too much.

Even though she's home alone, she closes the door to her bathroom and turns on the sink to drown out the sounds. She crouches over the toilet and sticks her fingers in her mouth. She gags, but nothing comes up. She tries using the opposite hand, she tickles the roof of her mouth, she reaches for her throat, she covers her fingers in soap so that the taste alone should be enough to make her gag.

She hasn't had this kind of trouble since the few feeble and halfhearted attempts she made before Janey taught her how to do it properly. She settles down, sitting cross-legged in front of the toilet.

It's okay, she tells herself, maybe I just need to relax for a minute. She takes a deep breath and tries again; again, she gags, she coughs, she spits, but no food comes up. She closes her eyes and leans against the wall opposite the toilet. Her fingers are still at her mouth, resting against her lips, reminding her to try again. She imagines that her stomach is clenching like a fist around the food she's eaten; she imagines her intestines snaking around tighter to hold everything in. She imagines that she—her fingers and her throat and her desire to throw up—is pitted against her greedy belly, and she feels outmatched.

So everything stays down. The bread with the nuts, the butter, the cheese, and the egg yolks. Her body just won't give it up.

**S**ETHIE'S CLASSMATES RETURN to school with skin tanned from vacations in exotic places like the Riviera Maya, St. Lucia, and Buenos Aires. Sethie goes back to school with a scar that peeks out of the top of her uniform skirt. Sethie likes her scar; it makes her feel dangerous, like she bought a fake ID over the break and used it to get a tattoo. She likes it even better than a suntan. A suntan isn't permanent.

Despite everything she ate on Sunday, she has lost six pounds; she was 110 when winter break began and is 104 now. She wonders if any of the weight lost was bled out of her when she cut herself, or when she picked at the scabs until she bled again. She wonders how much blood weighs and if it really matters because maybe your body just makes more blood to make up for what you lost. But maybe not, because then why would people need blood transfusions?

Sethie thinks she should have paid more attention in

biology; maybe then she'd know better about blood. She remembers one day in biology class they were made to find out their own blood type—this was in ninth grade—and the teacher had a little plastic stick that looked like a pen, except when she clicked the top of it a needle came out of its tip instead of a ballpoint. She remembers that when she was waiting in line for it to be her turn to have her finger pricked, the girls behind her were discussing the merits of regular versus low-fat versus nonfat salad dressing. Sethie had trouble following their talk. They were the popular girls, and Sethie was still skinny then; or, she still thought she was skinny then, or, really, she didn't yet think she was fat. She remembers that at the time, she'd never even tasted reduced-fat salad dressing, and she hardly even ate salads.

She remembers that she wondered why they didn't have the choice to opt out of this particular assignment; weren't some girls frightened at the sight of blood? Wasn't there anyone else who was scared about how much it might hurt when the needle pricked her? It's funny now, to think how scared she was then. She had been surprised at how little the needle hurt, didn't quite believe it; but now she knows that it hardly hurts at all, to break her own skin.

Her bra feels loose, but it's only six pounds she's lost, hardly enough to make a difference in how her bra fits.

On the first day back after break, Sethie's school has Health Day, when they sit you down and talk to you about self-awareness and stress levels, drugs and sex. Sethie thinks Health Day would be more useful if it were before finals, before everyone has studied their fingers to the bone, snorting their friends' Ritalin and Adderall to pull all-nighters. At least, she thinks, don't put Health Day on the first day back from Christmas break, when every other commercial on every other TV show is offering lessons on how to lose those stubborn holiday pounds.

In the morning, a victim of date rape gives a lecture. The entire upper school (at other schools it's called high school, but here at the White School, it's called upper school), grades nine through twelve, is packed into the assembly room. Sethie is the only senior who still sits on the floor rather than the faculty chairs. She knows she doesn't belong on the floor, but she wants to compare the feel of the hardwood to the way it felt before she lost six pounds. (Seniors are also allowed to take the elevators in second semester, but Sethie has vowed she won't do it. The stairs are such a great way to burn calories.) Sethie listens to the victim telling her story. It should be really moving, but Lifetime made a TV movie out of this particular victim's story, which nearly everyone in the senior class has already seen and from which the girl shows scenes as visual aids. When she's finished, the headmistress takes the podium to thank the girl for sharing her story. Sethie feels sorry for the girl, but in her mood, she also can't help thinking that this girl has parlayed her story into a fairly lucrative career, between the TV movie and the lectures. And the headmistress manages to turn her story into nothing more than a warning about why girls shouldn't drink at frat parties. Proper young ladies, she seems to imply, don't drink beer from a keg, and they certainly don't get date-raped.

Just before lunch, a nutritionist comes in to meet with the senior class. She is short—maybe 5'1"—and fit, and the shoulder pads on her suit make her look even smaller. Sethie recognizes the shoulder pads for what they are: an old, if unfashionable, trick to look thinner. She immediately hates the nutritionist for her hypocrisy: Don't worry about your bodies, girls, you're beautiful just the way you are—but it's okay for me to worry about how I look. After all, Sethie thinks, this nutritionist has her own lucrative career to worry about; this particular nutritionist appears regularly on the *Today* show, and everyone knows how important looks are in show business.

The nutritionist stands in front of the class and asks a question: "How many of you girls have ever said 'I feel fat'?"

Every single girl raises her hand.

"And how many of you girls actually believe that fat is a feeling?"

Not a single girl, not one, raises her hand. They're smart girls, good students; they know what's expected of them. But Sethie knows that most, or in any case many, of them would be perfectly capable of engaging in a debate about why fat is most definitely a feeling. Sethie shoots a look across the room at a girl named Alice. Alice is the class anorexic. Sure, there are plenty of girls in the class who've toyed with the disease, and with bulimia too. But Alice is the only one who really, Sethie thinks, deserves the title.

She was even sent to a rehab-type treatment center over the summer; she had to stay there, everyone knows, for three weeks. Sethie thinks maybe you're not a real anorexic until you need in-patient treatment. Alice is wearing a tank top, even though it's December and 32 degrees outside. Alice, Sethie knows, is proud of her thinness. Sethie stares at her in every class they have together.

Sethie decides to go to the bathroom, and then the nurse's office. She doesn't want to listen to the nutritionist; she made the same speech last year. Even the same opening question. Sethie bumps into Alice in the hallway.

"You needed out of there too, huh?" Alice asks.

"Can't stand that woman," Sethie says as they walk in step toward the nurse's office.

"Me either. She just repeats every single line in her book."

"You've read her book?" Sethie asks.

"Are you kidding? My parents shoved it in my face the minute it was published. Required reading, you know."

Sethie nods; there's no need to explain why Alice's parents were force-feeding her a book. It's probably the only luck they've ever had force-feeding her anything. Sethie's too intimidated by Alice to say anything more.

When they reach the nurse's office, Alice pulls a cigarette out of her jeans pocket.

"I'm gonna go out," she says. "Want to come?" Alice can get away with a lot, even brandishing a cigarette in a school hallway. If she ever gets caught, she just blames it on the stress of her disease, and the teachers feel bad for her.

Sethie shakes her head. "No thanks. Just gonna crash in here for a while." Sethie begins to turn, and she hits something hard: Alice's elbow.

"Sorry," Sethie says. Alice has dropped her cigarette; both she and Sethie bend down to retrieve it. Or in any case, Sethie intends to help pick the cigarette up for her, but instead she just watches Alice's right hand reach out for it. It seems impossible that Alice's fingers will be able to wrap around the cigarette. They're an odd shade of bluish white, and it doesn't seem that they could bend, let alone withstand the weight of anything at all, even a cigarette. Alice's fingers are so far apart that Sethie thinks a cigarette would just fall right through them anyway. They are lifeless fingers; for a moment, Sethie wishes that Alice would keep her hand still, reaching out, so that Sethie can hold hers up next to it and watch their hands side by side: Sethie's, pink with life; Alice's, blue and dead. But Alice moves, and her fingers wrap their way around the cigarette, and lift it off the ground.

Sethie smiles in apology; both girls stand up. Sethie hesitates by the nurse's door, watching Alice walk toward the exit. There is nothing delicate about Alice's thinness, nothing lithe and lovely, like Sethie wants to be. Alice's thinness reveals the effort behind it, in the way her bones battle her skin for room. Sethie can make out the ridges of her spine underneath her shirt. Sethie has always wanted defined shoulder blades; she has spent hours looking at pictures of actresses in backless dresses, trying to decide whose shoulder blades were the best. Alice's jut out like wings on her back. Sethie wonders whether it hurts, where the bones stick through the skin like that.

Alice will be cold, Sethie thinks, as she turns to walk into the nurse's office. She didn't stop to get a coat before heading outside. But then, Alice tends to smoke her cigarettes quickly—hungrily, Sethie thinks, cocking her head to the side—so she won't be outside for very long.

**T**HE NURSE SMILES at Sethie when she walks in; she's used to Sethie stopping by. Sometimes Sethie spends her lunch periods in here, chatting. The nurse's answer no matter what is wrong with you is that it must be because you haven't eaten breakfast. Sethie's often wondered why the nurse doesn't seem to mind that Sethie's constantly missing lunch.

The nurse doesn't question Sethie when she says she'd like to take a break from Health Day. Guess I didn't rest enough over break, Sethie explains, and the nurse nods sympathetically.

There are three beds in the nurse's office; one set of bunk beds and another plain twin bed. Sethie climbs into the upper bunk. The nurse reserves this bunk for the older girls only. It's up against a wall that's plastered with articles the nurse thinks will be useful to teen girls: safe sex and gynecology, peer pressure and menstrual cycles. Diagrams of how to put on a condom, insert a tampon, do a breast exam. And, of course, everywhere, there are articles about eating disorders. Articles that blame anorexia on Kate Moss and articles that blame bulimia on bad parenting. Articles that blame bad self-image on the fashion industry and a healthy self-image on any fashion models who actually look fit and healthy.

Sethie's read every single article over the years, and she can't find one to diagnose herself. They don't say whether you're anorexic if you only starve yourself some of the time. They don't say whether you're bulimic if you've only thrown up a handful of times. And they certainly don't allow for the fact that maybe, just maybe, a girl could be anorexic or bulimic simply because she hates being and feeling fat, rather than because of bad parents and trashy magazines. The only thing Sethie has ever gotten from these articles is tips on how to be better at dieting: one of them quotes a girl saying that she never ate a meal without drinking a cup of coffee first, to make her feel full. One of them tells the story of a bulimic who began eating with brightly colored foods, so she would know she could stop vomiting when she saw the colors come up. One of them quotes a girl who said celery speeds up your metabolism, because your body has to work harder to digest it. Sethie always wanted a more specific explanation for that one: how many more calories does celery burn, exactly; how much celery would she have to eat to make up for, say, a pint of frozen yogurt.

Sethie closes her eyes. She's not tired, not really; she just wanted to be alone. The nurse has turned off all the lights in the office except for the little one on her desk; she's really being very kind. Sethie thinks how different the nurse's job is for the lower schoolers, six-to-ten-year-olds with their sticky fingers and runny noses; the middle schoolers, getting their periods for the first time, too embarrassed to ask for a tampon or pad; and the upper schoolers, girls like Sethie who just need a quiet room where they can shut their eyes. Sethie listens to the sound of the nurse's fingers tapping her keyboard. It's a comforting sound, steady and clear.

The pillow has a piece of paper over it, like at a doctor's office, and Sethie wonders how often the sheets and blankets on these beds are washed. When Sethie turns onto her left side, the paper crackles beneath her head. Sethie presses her cheek against it; she expects it to be smooth, cool, but instead, it's rough and wrinkled, and when Sethie looks in the mirror later, there will be lines on her cheek where the paper was. Wrinkles, she'll think: this is what I will look like when I'm old.

Sethie imagines that the articles are looking down on her, arguing about her diagnosis, trying to decide which of them is right. She's bulimic, one says. No, anorexic, another argues, because bulimics are never as organized as she is. Yeah, but anorexics hate throwing up, another article counters.

Stop analyzing me, she begs the articles silently, and turns so that she's facing away from the wall. She closes her eyes, and the only thing that makes the buzz of the articles go away is thinking about Shaw.

Sethie imagines that Shaw is in this bed with her. She knows she should be angry at him, but she likes pretending he's there. Maybe it's a few years from now, and things have changed, and they're in school together, and they've gotten back together, and he's grown up into the type of boy who loves a girl like Sethie, the type of boy who tells her I love you all the time, just lying in bed watching TV, or studying side by side, or walking down the street. The type of boy who holds your hand and brings you a cup of coffee from Starbucks when you're too tired to get it yourself.

It might be easier, Sethie thinks, to just find a boy who's like that than to wait for Shaw to become one.

**S**ETHIE KNOWS THAT Ben is back at Columbia now. Classes haven't started yet—in college you have a longer winter break—but Ben has come back early; she's not sure exactly why, but he told her he'd be back around the fourth and now it's Monday the fifth, so Sethie is certain that he's back by now. She knows that Janey and Shaw are back in the city as well; their school started the same day White did. Maybe that's why Ben came back early; Doug was returning early because of Janey, and maybe Ben wanted to hang out with Doug. And maybe Ben and Doug are friends with Shaw's girl, Anna, and maybe she came back early too, to be with Shaw. Dating a high schooler sure complicates the schedule, she thinks.

Sethie decides she will call tonight; they have to watch *The Princess Bride,* after all, and it seems a shame not to have Ben see what 104 looks like. I should take 104 out for a spin, she thinks wryly; I should enjoy it while it lasts.

She waits until nine p.m. to call Ben. She's sitting on

her bed with the covers around her, but not pulled entirely over herself. After a couple of weeks of cooling and sweating herself, she can't tell whether she's hot or cold anymore. You expect metal to be cold, but the knife, which she has kept under her mattress, is always warm, and Sethie likes the way it feels. She holds the knife on her lap while she waits for Ben to pick up the phone. She likes the heft of it on her legs, like she has a pet sitting on her lap, keeping her company. She runs her finger along the top of it, like stroking a cat.

"Hello?"

"Jolly Green," Sethie says.

"I thought we'd discussed you'd never call me that," Ben says, and Sethie's stomach feels full because he has recognized her voice. She'd never have to eat again, she thinks, if she could always feel that full.

"I must have forgotten."

"Well, keep it in mind in the future."

"That I will."

"Good."

"How do you like being back in town?"

"I like it a lot better now," Ben says.

"Now?" Sethie asks.

"Now that you're coming over to watch *The Princess Bride*."

Sethie laughs; she hasn't laughed since before the holidays.

"Dude, that was so smooth."

"I thought you'd be impressed with it."

"I am."

"And?"

"And what?"

"And what time will you be on your way?"

"Tonight?"

"Yes, tonight—it's not too late, is it?"

"Not exactly. But some of us do have school tomorrow."

"Oh, of course, right."

Ben sounds so disappointed that Sethie says, "Screw it—give me twenty minutes and I'll be on my way, movie in hand."

Sethie imagines that Ben is grinning as he says, "See you soon," and hangs up the phone.

Sethie pulls on the skinny jeans she bought with Janey at Saks. She thinks back to that day—before they met Doug, before Shaw met Anna, probably, when she had only ever thrown up once and long before she took to hiding a knife under her bed. She thinks how tight these jeans seemed; she can't tell whether they're looser now because of the six pounds or whether it's just because the jeans have stretched from being worn. Sethie almost puts the knife in her purse before she leaves, but then she remembers that it's the movie she needs to bring.

She rolls down the windows of the taxi on her way uptown, practically sticks her head outside like a German shepherd. It's not quite raining out but not quite dry, and Sethie thinks that by the time she gets to Ben's her eyeliner will have begun to drip, but she doesn't roll up the window.

"Hey there, Happy New Year," Ben says as he opens the

frat house door. Sethie thinks that if only Ben had been in town for New Year's Eve, she would have gotten a midnight kiss.

"Happy New Year," she says back, leaning into him for a hug. He's so tall that her arms are around his hip bones. Sethie notices that they jut out, just like hers do when she's thin enough.

"I think you shrunk," Ben says, tousling her hair. "You look even littler than I remembered."

"Well, you look even taller than I remembered," Sethie says. But she thinks that she *has* shrunk; she is six whole pounds smaller, and she's proud that Ben has noticed, even now, when she still has on her coat, when you'd think it wouldn't even show.

She waits until they're in his room to unbutton her coat.

"Jesus Christ Sethie, you're supposed to gain weight over the holidays," Ben exclaims.

"Oh well." She shrugs. "I'm Jewish."

It's a good joke, and one she thinks Ben would normally laugh at, but he just takes her coat and asks for the movie.

The TV is across from his bed; it seems natural that they should be sitting on his bed, but Ben slides onto the floor, with his back against the bedframe, even though the room is so narrow that his feet hit the wall when his legs are only halfway straight. Sethie sits down beside him— there is room enough for her legs to be completely straight.

A few minutes into the movie, Sethie leans against Ben. She thinks maybe he'll put one of his long arms around her; it'd be more comfortable that way. But Ben is stiff beside her. She thinks maybe he's nervous, because maybe he wants to kiss her tonight. Maybe he's waiting until the movie is over, and maybe he can barely even pay attention to the movie; maybe he's too busy thinking about trying to kiss her afterward. She thinks maybe he won't be able to pay proper attention until she kisses him.

She tilts her face up, but he's so tall that even when she stretches so that she's sitting up straight, her lips can only reach his neck. So she begins there, by pressing her lips onto his neck. She can see just how it'll go; Ben will turn and his lips will fit on hers perfectly, and then it will be perfectly natural for her to lean back until she's lying on the floor, and he's on top of her. He'd hold himself up, though, because he is so much bigger than she is that if he really lay on top of her he might crush her. Sometime she'll have to ask him just how much he weighs; she suspects he might actually be twice her weight. As he leans over her, she'll make a joke that they have to pause the movie, and Ben will laugh, but he'll hardly be able to stop kissing her long enough to find the pause button.

Sethie closes her eyes as she presses her lips onto Ben's neck. She feels him begin to move, but instead of his lips pressed on hers, she feels his hand pressing on her shoulder. Pushing her away.

Sethie opens her eyes. It takes her a second to realize what's happened, because it looks so different from what she'd been expecting. Ben has pressed pause, and he's slid away from her, holding her at arm's length, which is very far away, considering his long arms.

183

Sethie blinks. "Why'd you pause the movie?"

"I think we need to talk."

"Okay."

Ben drops his hand from her shoulder. "Sethie, you look like hell."

Sethie is so surprised she actually can't stop her mouth from dropping open.

"I do?"

"Have you eaten a thing since I saw you before break? Have you slept?"

"What? I slept." It was, she thinks, the thing she probably did most of.

"And eaten?"

"Of course I've eaten."

"You don't look like you have."

"Ben, don't be ridiculous. A person can't just stop eating for two weeks." It sounds like such a reasonable point.

"Well, you didn't eat enough. Look at you. You're tiny."

Sethie doesn't say anything, but Ben looks at her like she's just said something awful.

"Sethie," he says softly, "you're smiling."

Am I? Sethie thinks. She finds she has to think about it, to stop and try to feel whether her own mouth is open, whether her lips have curled up. Of course she can't help smiling when someone says she's thin; even now, hurled at her as an accusation, it sounds like a compliment.

"Sethie, look, I like you. I think you know I do. But I think, right now, it might be better if we stayed friends."

"You just want to be friends?" Sethie stands up, and Ben does too. Suddenly, being small feels like a disadvantage. She considers standing on top of his bed to be at his eye level.

"Don't take it the wrong way."

"What's the right way?"

"I just don't think I'd be much use to you as a boyfriend right now."

"Much use?"

"I think you could use a friend more."

"You're not so much older than I am."

"What?"

"You're not so much older than I am that you have all this wisdom. I'm not your little high school case study."

"I know that." Ben runs his fingers through his hair, twisting the ends. He looks at the ceiling and says, "Sethie, don't be angry."

"So now you're not only telling me whether or not I should have a boyfriend, you're also telling me how I should feel about your telling me whether or not I should have a boyfriend?"

Ben sits down again, on the bed this time. Even sitting, he's nearly as tall as she is standing.

"I think I should leave," Sethie says finally.

"Okay. But I'd like to call you tomorrow."

"Why?"

"Because I'm your friend. And because eventually, you're going to get over this thing you're going through and then I'll probably want to be more than just your friend."

Sethie leans over him to retrieve her coat from the bed behind him.

"Well, you can't call me tomorrow. I never gave you my number, and I'm certainly not giving it to you now."

"Your number's in my phone," Ben says, like it's obvious. Which, she supposes, it is. She's called him a few times now.

"Well," she says, "delete it."

Sethie stands out on the corner to get a cab alone, even though it's late. She remembers the night when she and Ben met, how he and Janey both protested that she shouldn't be out on the streets by herself to catch a cab. She thinks now that Ben didn't really mean it. But then, after she's lowered herself into a cab and is slamming the door behind her, she thinks she can see the shadow of a giant looming on the corner, like maybe it followed her and hid behind her, and waited until she was safely inside a taxi to turn around and head back home.

**T**HE SECOND DAY of school, Sethie thinks, is probably a little early to start cutting class. And, she thinks, your second semester senior year is probably a little late to start cutting class. Sethie has never cut a class in her life, never had a grade below a B+, and has always been a favorite among her teachers. They'd never guess she's also a girl who's done drugs, and cut herself, and they certainly don't seem to notice that she's shrinking in front of them. They trust her so much that they believe her when she says she can't speak up in class this week because her doctor diagnosed her with pre-laryngitis. They trust her so much that when she asks to leave French class early to go home, the teacher sends her home with a packet of her favorite French cure-all tea.

The streets are pretty empty at 2 p.m. on a Thursday when everyone else is in school. Sethie's coat is unbuttoned, but she's wearing a hat and scarf; she's still not quite sure what the temperature is. She remembers something

Janey told her, a few weeks ago. Janey started doing yoga in November, and she said that since she started, the cold hasn't been bothering her, and it's because—she said—of her new muscles. Janey explained that when you work out, your muscles rip, and when you're resting, they're repairing themselves, which burns calories and keeps you warmer. Janey invited Sethie to come to yoga class with her, but Sethie turned her down. Sethie doesn't want to exercise, the same as she doesn't actually want to diet. She wants to be one of those girls who can eat whatever she wants and not gain weight, who can eat whatever she wants and not have to exercise for a taut stomach or arms, who can eat whatever she wants and so isn't tormented by a plate of fries or a bag of chips.

But because of what Janey has said about muscles keeping you warm, Sethie wonders now whether she was wrong in thinking that Shaw was strong and muscular; if he was really so muscular, maybe he wouldn't have been so constantly cold. But then, Sethie didn't believe Janey that building muscle really did burn calories, so maybe she was wrong about the warmth, too. The only way to lose any real weight is to eat less, Sethie thinks. And then less, and then less.

Sethie isn't sure where to go, now that she's out of school. Her mother worked late last night, and might have stayed home today to make up for it; the law firm only pays her to work a certain amount of hours. Even though her mother would probably believe she was sick just as easily as her French teacher did, she doesn't feel like having to repeat her lie. So she begins walking south; she begins walking in the direction of Shaw and Janey's school. She walks slowly, with her head down, her hat falling over her eyes, so that she almost walks into the boy who says, "Sethie!" a block away from Shaw's school.

Sethie looks up. It's Matt Ellison, who goes to school with Shaw and Janey, who came over to the vacant apartment to smoke up on the first day of school, with whom she crammed into a cab on the way up to Columbia.

"What are you doing out?" Matt asks, taking a step closer to her.

Sethie shrugs. She doesn't think Matt really has any business asking, since he should be in school, too.

Matt grins, like he's just remembered something. "Hey," he says, "that apartment still free?"

"What?"

"That apartment in your building—is it still available?"

"Oh, yeah. The new people haven't moved in yet." The doorman told her the new family would be moving in next week.

"Come with me," Matt says, offering his hand and pulling her toward Fifth Avenue.

"My building's in the other direction," Sethie says, resisting his pull.

"Yeah, but we just gotta meet someone first."

"Oh," Sethie says, understanding. They have to get the pot. Sethie's never actually seen anyone buy the drugs she's taken; certainly, she's never bought any of her own. They always seemed to just be there; there always seemed to be someone who knew better than she did where they came from and how to get there.

She follows Matt as he crosses Fifth Avenue and heads into Central Park. She sits down next to him on a bench just south of the Met. She wonders how long they have to wait.

"My buddy goes to school across town," Matt explains. "I told him I'd meet him in the park."

Sethie nods.

"You must be freezing."

"Not really."

"Well, you should button up anyhow," Matt says, and Sethie does as she's told.

Buying drugs, Sethie discovers, is kind of anticlimactic. Matt's friend shows up and gives him a brown paper bag that looks like it's more likely to have a bagel in it than a dime bag. Matt gives him forty dollars. And Sethie stares at the bag as they walk back to her apartment, thinking not about the pot, but about the bagel she can picture inside it.

"At least it's warm in here," Matt says, sliding his coat off. He opens the bag and takes out a can of Coke and a sandwich. Sethie looks up at him, confused.

Matt grins and says, "Let's just say you should wait before you take a bite out of the sandwich."

He gets up and goes into the kitchen. Sethie hears the pop of the soda can opening, and hears the liquid being poured down the drain of the sink. She's not sure whether the sink is currently hooked up to any pipes.

When Matt comes back, he's crushed a dent in the can and pulled a pen from his pocket to poke holes into it; he opens up the sandwich and pulls out the dime bag. Sethie wonders why it's called a dime bag when he paid forty bucks for it.

"Perfect, huh? You've got your munchie-maker and your munchie-snack in one convenient package."

Sethie smiles, even though the joke sounds disgusting to her. Some mayonnaise is sticking to the plastic bag out of which he shakes the pot. He places it delicately over the holes he's poked in the Coke can.

"Ladies first," he says, pulling out a lighter and passing the can to Sethie. She places her lips around the pop top, and Matt lights the weed. She inhales.

She hasn't smoked pot in weeks; she hasn't smoked without Shaw in months. Which is why, perhaps, the pot makes her want to curl up against someone. So she curls up against Matt, and why she kisses him when he tilts his head over hers, and why she lays down beneath him when he lies on top of her.

Matt is skinny—lanky, like Ben, but not as tall. When he pulls off her tights, Sethie thinks, Well, at least someone will see what 104 looks like. He does some of the same things that Shaw used to do, things that she liked: he presses his knee high between her legs, and kisses her neck below her ear. But he does things that Shaw never did, too, things that feel good: he pulls her arms to his mouth and kisses her wrists, and he kisses behind her knee.

Their hip bones knock against each other with

repeated thuds and Sethie wonders whether her bones might crack, as though she were old, with brittle bones and papery skin. Older people, she thinks, don't seem to sweat. Their skin seems so dry that maybe they don't get dirty, maybe they don't have an odor to them aside from the odors of the lotions they rub onto their sore muscles and the medicines they take and the cleaning solutions used around them.

Sethie isn't sweating. In fact, by the time Matt rolls off of her, she is cold. Well, that's something, she thinks, at least I can feel temperatures again. But then that could just be the pot.

"Wow," Matt says, panting. "This is the best class I ever cut."

Sethie thinks that sentence doesn't really mean anything; he means this is the best time he ever had cutting class.

Matt says, "I shouldn't say it, but I've been thinking about it ever since you and Shaw broke up."

"What?" Sethie says, surprised.

"I know, it's a lame thing to say. But it's the truth." He slides over to sit next to her. Sethie sees that his pants are still around his ankles and she thinks that he might get a splinter in his ass, sliding over the hardwood floor like that. She knows she's supposed to lean her head on his chest, but now that she's cold she really just wants to get dressed and go into her room, get under her covers. At least she kept her shirt on so he couldn't see the scar on her belly to ask questions about it, even if that means Matt didn't get to see how much flatter her stomach has gotten.

She knows she's supposed to feel bad about what happened; upset that she had sex with some guy she barely knows and certainly doesn't care about. But at this moment, she's smiling. At least Matt called it a breakup.

**S**ETHIE CONSIDERS CHARGING her phone again. Her mother might begin to wonder, now that school has started and her friends are, ostensibly, all back in town, why the phone never rings and why Sethie never leaves her room except to go to school. She even eats, when she does eat, in her bedroom: her latest plan allows her to have three things: granola with yogurt, carrots with mustard, and chicken salad from the store across the street. She thinks that she can trick her body into thinking she's eating more than she is if she eats food with different textures: the creamy yogurt with the granola; the crunchy carrots and the smooth mustard; the mashed-up chicken with the hard pieces of onion and celery.

Sethie doesn't actually like yogurt, but she read that the active cultures help keep your stomach flat, so she added it to her diet like it was medicine she ought to take. She tells herself that since she doesn't like it, it should be easier to leave some over when she eats it; since she doesn't like it, it should make her full faster, because she can't possibly be hungry for something she doesn't think tastes good. For every spoonful she eats, she must leave some yogurt on the spoon, so that even when she's finished, there is still a tiny bit of yogurt left. She is so careful to load each spoonful properly that it takes her twenty minutes to eat one serving of yogurt with granola. Sometimes, she finishes the whole thing despite herself; then she feels like she's failed. It's almost funny, she thinks: little kids get praise from their parents when they clean their plates. She can't quite remember when the goal became the exact opposite of itself.

Her father might call. She hasn't spoken to him since before the holidays; he told her he sent her a Christmas check. She told him it was technically a Hanukkah check, and he'd laughed. Sethie laughed too; she wasn't sure why it was funny, but it seemed easier to laugh than to acknowledge that she and her father don't know each other very well at all. She hasn't seen him for nearly a year, though that's not because she's been avoiding him; it's because she wanted to spend the summer with Shaw this year, instead of in California with her dad.

She imagines what the first day of school might have been like, this year, if the teachers had asked for "What I did on my summer vacation" essays the way that they did in elementary school. She imagines an essay about sheets that smelled like pot and sex, because Sethie and Shaw didn't know how to work the fancy washing machine at his parents' country house. She thinks she could have written a full essay about nothing more than rationing out Ritz crackers every day; about the taste and crumble of each cracker she allowed herself to eat, about the guilt when she ate more than she should have.

Sethie decides to keep her phone charged. At least she knows that Ben won't call. And she can screen everyone else.

Janey calls every night at seven o'clock and sometimes again at ten. She has even tried calling the senior lounge, Sethie knows, because of the messages scrawled on the whiteboard next to the pay phone: Sethie, Janey called; Sethie, call Janey; Sethie, Janey says Hi.

Sethie doesn't think she ever gave Janey the number for the pay phone in the senior lounge, but she guesses that it would be easy enough for Janey to get it. Surely plenty of people at Janey's school have friends at White who gave them the number. Or maybe some of the boys there have girlfriends here; Sethie knows now that plenty of people really do use those words—*boyfriend* and *girlfriend*—after all. Sethie thinks that maybe Janey is calling just on the off chance that Sethie will be the one to pick up eventually.

Sometimes, in the messages Janey leaves on her voice mail, Sethie can hear Doug's voice in the background. Janey must be calling from his room at the frat house, the room just above Ben's room. Sometimes she thinks that Ben must be in the room with Janey when she calls, that he's told Janey about how she threw herself at him, that he wants nothing to do with that fucked-up high school girl from the Upper East Side.

Sethie should not, then, be surprised on a Saturday

morning, two weeks after school has started, when Janey shows up in her room. Sethie is still in bed, under the covers. She isn't sleeping, and she isn't reading or watching TV. She isn't even thinking. She's just staring at the ceiling, like she's waiting for something to happen. Well, she thinks, Janey's arrival is certainly something.

"Hey," Janey says.

Sethie rolls over to look at Janey; there is snow slowly melting off the tips of Janey's hair, as though she'd walked over with a hat on, but the bottom ends of her hair stuck out from under it. Sethie hadn't known it was snowing; her blinds are shut tight. It hasn't snowed this winter yet, not once. She'd kind of forgotten about the possibility of snow, or even rain, when she was so busy concentrating on keeping warm, and keeping cold. Keeping dry hadn't even occurred to her.

"Don't you knock?"

"I didn't think you'd answer. I mean, why would you be any more likely to answer a knock than a phone call?"

Janey glances over at Sethie's cell phone resting on the table next to the bed. "Have you even listened to any of my messages?" she asks.

"I've listened to them all." Sethie rolls onto her back, and focuses her eyes on the ceiling.

Janey picks up Sethie's phone and sees that there are messages Sethie hasn't played yet. "Doesn't look like it," she says.

"I've listened to most of them," Sethie says. "They all pretty much say the same thing."

"Oh."

Sethie's lying. She's actually waiting to listen to Janey's most recent messages until sometime later today; she's saving them.

She rolls over again to look at Janey. Janey pulls her hair back into a ponytail, using the rubber band she always wears around her wrist like a bracelet. Sethie thinks of the way rubber bands feel tight on her own wrists, and how this one practically dangles on Janey's. Janey's wearing jeans with a scoop-neck top. She sits down in Sethie's desk chair, across from the bed.

"You have the best collarbone," Sethie says finally.

"What?" Janey slouches now, as if she's trying to hide her collarbone.

"Your collarbone. It stands out just like a collarbone is supposed to, straight across your chest. Mine doesn't stand out, no matter how much weight I lose."

"It has nothing to do with how much I weigh. It's genetics. It's just the way I'm built, I guess."

"I guess," Sethie says, rolling back over. She'd prefer if Janey would take credit for her collarbone. "Where's your coat?"

"What?"

"Your coat, your hat, your scarf, your gloves?"

"In the living room. Your mom took them."

"She did?"

"Yeah, how'd you think I got into the apartment?"

"I thought maybe I'd left the door unlocked or something. I kind of forgot my mother was there."

"She's there. She says she's barely left the house the last couple of weeks. She says she's been leaving work early to make sure she's here when you get home from school. She says she's scared to leave you alone."

Sethie considers this; she doesn't think it makes a difference, whether her mother is home or not, because either way, Sethie stays behind her bedroom's closed door.

"Since when do you talk to my mom?" she asks Janey.

"She asked me to come here."

"She did? I didn't know she even knew who you were."

"Well, she did. And I'm glad she did."

"Why?"

"Because you won't return my calls. Because the last time I showed up here, you wouldn't even open the front door all the way. At least your mom let me in."

"How'd she find you?"

"She called my mom."

"I've never met your mom."

Janey shakes her head. "I'd never met yours."

"Where'd she get your number?"

Janey shrugs. "I don't know."

"Why did she call you?"

"She said she was worried about you. She said you won't talk to her."

"It's not that I won't talk to her. I just never see her."

"She says you walk away from her every time she comes near you. She says every time she opens her mouth to say something to you, you close your bedroom door behind you."

Sethie thinks about this. She can remember seeing her mother over the past several weeks, passing by her in the kitchen, or on the way from the front door to her bedroom. If she thinks about it, she can remember her mother's open mouth, and the way she'd rush into her bedroom before any words could come out of it.

"She's freaking out because you're not eating. She says she took you out to lunch before school started just to see if she was overreacting, and you barely ate anything."

"I ate and ate."

"That's not what she said. She said it was painful, watching you eat. She said you tore the bread into little pieces and only ate the crumbs. She said you'd put butter on your knife and then spread it over the bread, like holding the knife above it, so the butter didn't actually touch the bread."

Sethie thinks for a minute; that's not how she remembers brunch at all. She remembers the butter on her knife, and the bread with the nuts and the raisins. She remembers breaking the bread into pieces. She remembers lifting the bread to her mouth. But she can't quite remember the crunch of nuts between her teeth, or the taste of butter on her tongue.

"Sethie?" Janey prompts.

"I'm eating," Sethie insists. She thinks about the granola, the yogurt, the chicken salad. And she realizes, also, that the kitchen has never lacked a single one of these items, not for weeks now, or maybe even months. Has her mother been watching what she'll eat? Has she been filling the kitchen with foods that she knows Sethie eats, because she's scared that one day, if Sethie can't find the thing she wants in the kitchen, she simply won't eat at all?

"Not much from the look of you," Janey says.

"What?"

"I said you're not eating much, not from the look of you."

Sethie shrugs.

"Wipe that grin off your face. Jesus, Sethie," Janey says, and Sethie looks down. "I can't believe I actually played a part in this."

"What do you mean?"

Janey takes a deep breath. "I'm so sorry I taught you how to throw up. I don't know what I was thinking. I think I was just . . . I was showing off for you. I wanted to be your friend."

"It's not your fault. I would have figured out how to do it eventually anyway."

"I just wish I'd never done it."

"It's okay. It's not your fault."

Janey looks away. Sethie thinks maybe she's trying not to cry. Today, Janey is not wearing her usual smudged eyeliner and her lips are dull and chapped instead of shining under their usual layer of Vaseline. She's pulled her legs up onto the chair so that her chin is resting on her knees, and she is biting at the sides of her fingernails thoughtfully, as if she is trying to do a good job at biting her nails. She looks, Sethie thinks, very young; maybe even younger on her chair than Sethie looks in her bed.

Eventually Janey says, "I screamed at Shaw on Monday. I yelled so hard my throat hurt."

Sethie can't imagine Janey yelling. Janey is always in control.

"What did he do, Sethie? He said you guys talked about it and that you were—his words—totally cool about Anna."

"I was totally cool about Anna."

"Obviously not," Janey says. "Look at you."

"I was. I was so cool about it that I slept with him."

"What?"

"I slept with him."

"After you found out he was cheating on you?"

"He wasn't cheating. We were just friends with benefits, everybody knew that."

"Everybody but you," Janey says, but she says it tenderly, like maybe it wasn't Sethie's fault for not having known it.

"He said it was nice to do it one last time, to say good-bye to the physical part of our friendship."

Janey laughs, which makes Sethie sit up. When she sits up, the covers fall down around her waist, and Janey can see how thin Sethie is now; Sethie is wearing only a tank top and boxer shorts. She has lost two more pounds since school started: 102.

"You call that an undefined collarbone?" Janey says. She sounds angry, and Sethie lies back down and pulls the covers back around her. Janey stands up and walks over to the bed. For a second, Sethie thinks she's going to rip the covers back, to get a closer look at how skinny she is. But instead, Janey leans down and pulls off her shoes, big cold-weather boots into which she'd tucked her jeans, and then she does pull back the covers, but only enough so that she can slide between them, and curl up next to Sethie.

Sethie inhales sharply. She thinks that maybe Janey will be able to feel the knife under her mattress, like the Princess in the story of the Princess and the Pea.

"There's a knife under the mattress," Sethie says.

"What for?" Janey says, like it's no big deal.

"I like it. It makes me feel calm."

"Like in *Gone with the Wind*?"

"What?"

"In *Gone with the Wind,* Butterfly McQueen said if you put a knife under the bed, it cuts the pain in half."

Sethie considers this; was that what she'd been doing with the knife, trying to make the pain smaller somehow?

Janey reaches over the side of the bed and pulls out the knife from underneath them.

"I'm going to confiscate this," Janey says, and Sethie thinks that Janey probably understands what the knife is really doing there.

"I have other knives. A whole kitchen full of them," Sethie says, not because she wants the knife back, but because she knows there are holes in Janey's plan. She doesn't see how Janey can protect her.

"Well, I'll confiscate those too," Janey says, like it's the easiest thing in the world, keeping Sethie away from all sharp objects. Sethie nods. Janey sounds so confident that she believes it.

Janey gets up and puts the knife in her purse, and

Sethie is relieved because that means she's taking it with her when she goes. Then Janey gets back into the bed, close to Sethie. She reaches under the covers and takes Sethie's hand, and Sethie notices that Janey's hand isn't cold like Shaw's, or hot like Ben's, but comfortably warm. Sethie feels like Goldilocks when she discovered the temperature of the porridge that was just right.

"So what else did he say, besides wishing a sweet farewell to your fun parts?"

Sethie can't help herself: she giggles.

"When I started crying, he kissed my tears."

"What an asshole."

"I thought it was sweet."

"Exactly what he wanted you to think. Shaw is such a loser. If you're going to break a girl's heart, have the balls to break it. But he has to feel like he's comforting you. You know that's an asshole's move, don't you?"

Sethie shakes her head.

"He's an asshole, Sethie. I promise you, anyone who heard this story would be able to see that."

"Well, I didn't know that," Sethie says.

"Listen, I know you're a mess right now, but I promise you, and I mean this in the nicest way possible: it happens all the time. This is what girls do when bad boys hurt them. Breakups hurt."

"It feels better when you call it a breakup. You're the second person to do it." Third, Sethie thinks, if she counts herself.

"Who was the second person?"

"Matt. From your class."

"When did you see him?"

"The other day. Around."

"I bet he came looking for you. He always had a crush on you."

Sethie smiles. It feels good, being the kind of girl that someone would have a crush on.

"Anyway," Janey says, "what else would you call it, other than a breakup?"

Sethie shrugs.

"Breakups hurt," Janey repeats. "Granted, you're taking it a little further than, you know, a normal girl might, but we're going to work on that."

And then I'll be normal? Sethie asks silently.

"Maybe *normal* isn't the right word. Normal isn't exactly something to strive for. But you know, healthy."

"Right," Sethie says, but she doesn't believe it, and Janey must be able to tell, because she says, "Yes, Sethie, healthy. You've got to figure this mess out, because you and I have so much fun ahead of us. We're going to both get into Columbia and rule the school. We're going to stay up all night writing A-plus papers and spend spring break someplace exotic. We're going to study abroad in Italy and eat gelato without counting calories. And, bonus, we already have these boys, these great boys—good guys—who will be waiting for us when we get there."

"When we get to Italy?"

"When we get to Columbia."

Sethie almost laughs, but instead she shakes her head.

For a few minutes, she'd managed to forget what had happened with Ben, but now she remembers. She thinks even if she does get into Columbia, she can't possibly go there, go to a place where she's already made such a complete fool of herself.

"What's the matter now?" Janey asks.

"Ben."

"Ben likes you. A boy like Ben is exactly what isn't the matter."

"No. Didn't he tell you what happened?"

"No. Though he did give me *The Princess Bride* to give back to you. It's in my bag."

"He didn't tell you?"

"Tell me what, Sethie?"

"I made a fool of myself."

"So? Ben won't care. He cares about whether you're healthy, not about whether you made a fool out of yourself in front of him. He's crazy about you. He's been asking about you every day."

"He's probably just worried about me, 'cause what girl wouldn't be a mess after what happened."

"He says he misses hanging out with you, actually. I swear, every time I come over he's looking behind me to see if you're there."

"I doubt it."

"Sethie, is it so hard for you to believe that he wants to be your friend? Even if you did make a fool out of yourself?"

"Who wants to be friends with a fool?"

"Dude, Sethie, way to be melodramatic," she says, and

Sethie laughs. "You always make me laugh. You make me feel . . ." Janey searches for a word and finally says, shrugging, "Special. You're special. That is, when you're not, you know, lying semi-suicidally in your bed for days on end."

"Guess I have to work on that part of my personality."

"Don't worry, we will." Janey laughs again. Sethie can feel the warmth from Janey's body spreading across the bed. "My God, Sethie, you need so much therapy," Janey says, but she's still laughing.

"I do?"

"Therapy or maybe a dog."

"A dog?" Sethie repeats, and now she's laughing too.

"Well, maybe not a dog, because he couldn't come live with us in the dorms."

Sethie stops laughing. "Oh crap."

"What now?"

"I can't go to Columbia."

"Sethie, I'm telling you, you got like a twenty-two-thousand on the SATs. I think you're getting in."

"No, I'm serious, I can't go."

"Why not?"

"Because Shaw's going to go. I don't want to go to the same school he's going to."

Janey starts laughing again, this time even harder. "Sethie, I really don't think you have to worry about that."

"Why not?"

"I know you go to a different school and everything, so maybe you couldn't tell just how much of Shaw's so-called intellectual prowess is just talk."

"Huh?"

"Sethie, there's no way Shaw's getting into Columbia, not with his grades."

"Really?" Sethie asks, and now she's laughing too, laughing because she can't believe on just how many different levels Shaw managed to trick her.

"Not a chance," Janey says.

**WHEN JANEY LEAVES**, Sethie walks her to the door, where they hug. Janey promises to call her later, and Sethie promises to pick up when she does. Walking to the door means walking through the living room, where Sethie's mother is sitting on the couch with a magazine in her lap.

"Your magazine's upside down," Sethie says. Rebecca snaps it shut.

Sethie knows the magazine was just a prop, just something for Rebecca to hold on her lap so maybe it wouldn't look like she was waiting to see her daughter come out of her room. Rebecca hasn't seen Sethie since she dropped to 102, at least not without her coat on. Sethie stands in front of her now in her tank top and shorts, and Sethie recognizes the look on her mother's face—she's seen it twice now, on Ben's face, and on Janey's. But when Rebecca makes the face, Sethie doesn't smile; instead, she begins to cry.

When Rebecca stands up, the magazine falls onto the

floor, and the sound of the pages hitting the rug is loud in Sethie's ears. Her mother's footsteps coming toward her are loud too, despite her mother's tiny feet. She can even hear the cloth of Rebecca's sweater brushing against her skin when Rebecca wraps her arms around her.

"I'm a mess," Sethie says.

"Yes," Rebecca says, "I've noticed."

"I didn't know you could tell," Sethie says.

"I've been watching."

Sethie nods. It isn't until her mother says that she's been watching that Sethie realizes she's been hiding.

"I'm ruining your sweater," Sethie says, and she disentangles herself from her mother's arms, takes a step back from her.

"I don't mind," Rebecca says, and Sethie notices that her voice is shaking.

"You sound nervous," Sethie says.

"I am," Rebecca says.

"Why?"

"Because I think this conversation that I'm about to have with you is going to be one of those very important conversations."

"Why?"

"Because I have to tell you that I know you haven't been sleeping without taking Valium. And I know you're smoking pot. And I know you haven't been eating."

"I've been eating," Sethie responds weakly, a reflex.

"Not enough."

"Not enough," Sethie repeats, surprising herself.

"I have to tell you that I think you need help, and I have to tell you that if you disagree with me, I'm going to have to tell you that I don't care about your opinion."

"You don't care about my opinion?"

"Not if it's that you don't need help. Actually," Rebecca interrupts herself, "I do care if you tell me that. I care very much. Because if you tell me that, then I know that you're even more far gone than I realized. So I want you to tell me: do you think you need help?"

Sethie considers the question. She takes a few steps away from her mother, to the couch. She sits down. She considers her life before she began dating Shaw; she considers the life she'd like to have dating Ben, or at least a boy like him, a boy who is sweet, a boy who even wanted her first. She considers what it would be like to go to Columbia with Janey, and she considers what she will need to do to go there. She considers the past two weeks of her life, she considers the months and maybe years she's spent hating her body. She thinks about lying on the floor beneath Matt, a perfectly nice guy she had no business sleeping with; she thinks about Alice, the bluish tinge of her fingers, her shoulder blades ugly on her back. Sethie looks at her mother.

"You look tired," Sethie says.

"I am tired," Rebecca answers.

"Because of me?"

Rebecca nods. "Being this scared is exhausting," she says, and she almost smiles.

Sethie nods; she sees the fear on Rebecca's face; she

thinks of the horrified way Janey balked when she saw her hip bones between her T-shirt and her boxer shorts, remembers how disgusted Ben looked when he saw her last. She can't remember the last time she asked Janey how English class was going, the last time she asked Ben if he ever convinced his frat brothers to stop making him their handyman. Sethie wonders when she became so selfish.

Then she thinks about the feisty girl on the phone with Ben; the girl laughing with Janey; the girl confidently taking her SATs and filling out her college applications. She thinks about acceptance envelopes in the mailbox, shopping for sheets and pillows for her dorm room. It sounds simple, but the truth is, she wants to do all of those things more than she wants to hide in her bedroom, maybe even more than she wants to lose weight.

"Well," Sethie says finally, "I think I need something."

Rebecca smiles. "That's a start."

Yes, Sethie thinks, it's a start.

. . . WORK IT OUT YOUR OWN WAY.
HAVE GOOD LUCK AT YOUR AGE.

—*Ernest Hemingway*
"Lines to a Girl 5 Days After Her 21st Birthday"

# ACKNOWLEDGMENTS

**I WAS ABOUT HALFWAY** through reading Alice Hoffman's beautiful book *Blackbird House* when an image popped into my head: a girl, still as a stone, crouched beside a toilet. She could have been one of hundreds, thousands of girls who make themselves throw up. She could have been me, during a number of years in my life when sticking my fingers down my throat didn't feel at all counterintuitive, when I believed that starving myself was the only reasonable and effective way to lose weight.

Later that day, I saw that girl again, but this time I knew her name: it was Sarah Beth Weiss. At once, I knew everything about her. I wanted so badly to tell her that she wouldn't always feel like she did now. I wanted to tell her that someday she wouldn't hate her own flesh, that she would eat without fear; that someday there would be a man she couldn't even imagine who would love her and whom she would love better than she'd dreamed. I wanted to tell her all of that, but I couldn't. What I could do, and what I began to do that day, was write her story.

I wrote this book both reluctantly and eagerly, both inevitably and willingly—and, as always, with a great deal of help.

Many thanks to my magnificent agent and teacher, Sarah Burnes, who loved Sethie from the start, and who always understands exactly what it is I'm trying to say and guides me to say it better. Thanks also to Logan Garrison, Rebecca Gardner, Will Roberts, and the entire team at Gernert.

Many thanks to my lovely and amazing editor, Erin Clarke, for her tireless support, guidance, and patience. Thanks to Melissa Greenberg for the stunning cover. Thanks to my entire Random House family, including Nancy Hinkel, Kathy Dunn, and Chip Gibson, and all my good friends in marketing, publicity, and sales.

Many thanks to *The Stone Girl*'s earliest readers, Jessica DePaul and Rachel Feld; and thanks always for your creative input, Ranse Ransone. Many thanks to my remarkable circle of friends. Thanks to whatever magical trick of fate it was that made me, after years of refusing to work out, decide to try yoga, and thanks to Mindy Ferraraccio for being my teacher and friend.

Thank you to my parents, Elaine and Joel; my sister, Courtney; my grandmother Doris; and to the Gravitts and the Getters.

And thank you for everything, JP Gravitt.

ALL KNOWLEDGE, THE TOTALITY OF ALL QUESTIONS
AND ALL ANSWERS, IS CONTAINED
IN THE DOG.

—*Franz Kafka*